Got the Life
A Nicki Sosebee Novel

JADE C. JAMISON

Copyright © 2013, 2011 Jade C. Jamison

All rights reserved.

ISBN: 147006605X
ISBN-13: 978-1470066055

CHAPTER ONE

WHY DO ALL the bad boys have to be so fucking cute? Nicki Sosebee sat on a hard wooden pew in the Winchester County courthouse, shifting to relieve the pressure on her bottom. She lifted her pencil up off the stenographer's notebook she'd been writing notes in and tapped the eraser against the paper. She shook her head. He might've been a bad boy, but he was sure nice to look at.

The accused, a Mr. Jason Edwards, sat at the defendant's table, a smirk etched on his flawless face. His dark brown eyes smoldered, and his light brown hair was spiked, but it was too short to seem extreme. What made Nicki feel warm all over, though, were his arms full of tattoos. For a reason she could never explain, she thought body modifications made guys look…well, hot. And Edwards? Well, he was of the four hundred degrees Fahrenheit variety.

When Edwards first walked in the courtroom, the judge reprimanded him for not wearing proper courtroom attire.

It indicated he wasn't taking the proceedings seriously. Edwards had sneered but said nothing. Nicki knew the man had saved himself a contempt of court citation by biting his tongue—she'd sat in Judge Lewis's courtroom before, and he didn't let flippant remarks pass. One sarcastic statement and Edwards would have found his arraignment continued, his ass back in the same lame jail cell he was in just a few minutes ago. Instead, he'd likely walk out of the courtroom in just a few minutes, along with a date for a hearing. But hearing or no, he'd be a free man—temporarily, at least. His court-appointed attorney simply apologized and promised it wouldn't happen again.

Nicki felt compelled to follow this case…and it wasn't just because Edwards was nice to look at. It didn't matter that a good many defendants she saw day in and day out in this courthouse were recovering meth addicts (some of them *weren't* recovering and didn't plan to anytime soon, however) who were nothing but bones and sunken cheeks or old alcoholics with lined foreheads and red noses. That was beside the point. No, instead it was because his case was something *different*. And different stories were the kind her editor would publish. He didn't give a shit about the ordinary. Ordinary stuff found a small corner in the paper, if that, but the different stuff? Sometimes it could even wind up on the front page.

That hadn't happened to Nicki. Yet. That was one of her short-term goals.

Nicki didn't have many long-term goals. She didn't like to think that far into the future. Talk about pressure. She liked the way a lot of her Zen friends approached life, living in the moment. She knew her own refusal to think too far ahead had nothing to do with Buddhism, but it was a good reason to give people when they asked. Really, though, she knew it was something else that kept her from looking too far, and if she wasn't ready to face it, she certainly wasn't ready to talk about it.

She bit her lip as she caught herself staring at the half blank page on her lap. She had to pay attention to what was happening in the courtroom. Can't have a front page story if you don't get the facts straight. She adjusted in the pew again and paid attention to the proceedings. She managed to catch the defendant pleading "not guilty" and scribbled it down on the pad in her lap. Then she heard the low rumble of her cell phone vibrating in the pew next to her, indicating that she had an incoming call. She picked it up and looked at the screen. It was Sean. She noted it but set it back on the seat. He could wait.

The judge gave a date for the defendant's next hearing and set bail at $25,000. Edwards was taken into custody and escorted out of the courtroom. Well, she'd been wrong that he would get to walk, but it made his case all the more interesting. The judge must see Edwards as a risk, meaning this case was important enough to cover in the paper. Nicki jotted the date and amount and saw an entire row of people—Edwards's family, she assumed—make gestures and mutter amongst themselves. They didn't get loud enough for the judge to reprimand them, but she looked them over and wrote a couple of details for herself. Just as she looked up from the paper again, she saw her cell phone screen light up again. She pressed a couple of buttons to read the text message. *Call me*, the screen beckoned her. Nicki's right eyebrow curled—Sean *never* texted. What was up with that? She sat through the next few arraignments of the morning—nothing big to report on, but those cases would probably be clumped together in a little paragraph all their own somewhere in the paper tomorrow. *Those* details weren't her problem. Her problem was finding a story good enough to make the front page. And she thought Jason Edwards's tale of family loyalty, criminal mischief, and four counts of arson might be the one. She planned to write a small blurb soon for the online edition of the *Winchester Tribune* and tomorrow morning's paper edition. Then it was up to Neal Black, the editor of her hometown paper, to decide if it was good enough to print.

She walked out of the courtroom into the cool, marble-floored hallway and quickly found her way outdoors. Ugh. It was hot outside. Arizona hot. *It shouldn't be this fucking hot in the Colorado foothills*, Nicki thought. She began walking down the concrete steps to the sidewalk and decided she'd better go see Sean. Something important *must* have been going on for Sean to call and then text. She'd better put him out of his misery ASAP.

CHAPTER TWO

NICKI LEANED HER back against a wooden table in Sean's garage. Sean was tinkering on a motorcycle while talking to Nicki. Nicki was looking over at the most precious thing in the world to Sean: his custom-built Harley. He hardly ever rode the damn thing, but it was souped up, and he was constantly doing more to it, which was why its permanent home was in his shop. It was chrome and black with red here and there and contained over one hundred horses in its engine. But looking at that beauty couldn't help Nicki concentrate. She was biting the side of her cheek, forcing herself to not say a word until she knew she could be calm. *Anything you say can and will be used against you.* Nicki tried to pay attention to Sean's next words but found it difficult. *Jesus.* She couldn't believe what she was hearing. He must have gone and lost his fucking mind.

He had a blue bandanna tied around his head like he usually did when he worked in the shop, covering that gorgeous head of dark blonde just-a-little-too-long hair. He kept looking up from the bike to make eye contact with her, those dark blue orbs piercing into her.

"Wait," Nicki said. "Did I hear you right?"

Sean looked up from the bike, setting the wrench down on the small bench. "Yeah. Kayla wants us to move in together. But I wanted to see what you thought."

Nicki shook her head and raised her eyebrows. "Why don't you ask your guy friends what *they* think?"

Sean smiled that killer smile of his, his perfect white teeth disarming her. "You know why. Because they're a bunch of insensitive assholes. Besides, even if they weren't, they'll tell me I'm pussywhipped even if they'd do the same thing."

Nicki smirked. "Well, they're right. You *are* pussywhipped."

He sighed and picked up a socket wrench. "Is that what you really think?"

God, she was pissed at him, but there was no way in hell she was going to show it. She wasn't angry that he was thinking about moving in with his girlfriend. No, she was pissed that he was making her talk to him about it. But she had to be cool. "What do *you* want to do, Sean? Do you *want* to move in with her?"

He shrugged his shoulders while sliding a socket on his wrench. "I don't know. That's why I need your advice."

Nicki walked closer to the bike between them. "Do you love her?"

Sean resumed fidgeting with the bike, working the noisy socket wrench, and wouldn't make eye contact with Nicki. "I don't know. Maybe that's part of it too?"

He was worse than a girl. "Would you marry her?"

"God, Nicki, why are you asking me all this shit?"

"Because those are the things *I* would consider before moving in with someone." She walked over to the bench and sat next to him. He finally looked over at her. "What are *you* thinking about?"

He looked down at the tool in his hand, then looked in her eyes. "Well, it would save on rent, that's for sure. And we spend a lot of time together already, so there's that. And it would be nice to come home to her arms and a hot cooked meal." So he wanted a slave. Or ready sex. Or both.

But she sensed that he was wanting a reason to tell Kayla no. And Nicki refused to be the bad guy. If he didn't want to do it, he needed to find those reasons within himself. "But…?"

She heard his exhale. "But…I don't know that I want to be around her 24/7. I've seen what it does to other people. I mean, Christ. You might as well get married if you're gonna move in together."

Why had she decided to sit down next to him? She could hardly stand being this close, seeing the perfect cut of his longish soul patch and sideburns trimmed into not quite mutton chops, not quite a chinstrap beard but certainly longish sideburns, larger than most guys wore them, highlighting the sexy shape of his angled jaw. Sean had always been all about looking good and it drove Nicki crazy. She hoped he didn't know she still thought about him that way. *Of course he doesn't, dumbass.* Why would he ask her about his girlfriend if he thought she still cared? He'd only do it if he was an asshole. And he wasn't. Usually. At least, he wasn't being one right now. Nicki was fairly certain of that.

She stood and cleared her throat, smoothing her denim miniskirt with her hands. "Well, I hate to tell you this, but I can't help you. I feel like any advice I give you will be wrong."

Sean stood up, facing her, leaving the socket wrench on the bench. He grinned. "No worries. You helped."

God, it was no wonder she couldn't get over him. Not only was he smart and fun with a great sense of humor, he was nicer to look at than an entire night of buff WWE wrestlers with their shirts off. He was wearing a simple white tee and faded blue jeans, but she could make out the definition of his chest. There was nothing soft about Sean. And his arms were well-inked, mostly in black with very little color. Even the fingers of his right hand were tattooed between his knuckles—each finger had one letter that spelled *BAMF*. He said it was his punching hand, so when he'd throw a right cross in a bar brawl, the recipient would know who took him down. She remembered when her parents first saw the tattoo and asked him what it meant. Her mother was *not* amused to discover that Sean considered himself one BadAss MotherFucker. Too bad for mom he couldn't just cover it up. But she seemed to get used to it after a while. In that way, Sean managed to have Nicki's mother captivated too. Nicki sighed. "If you say so." She wondered what his decision was going to be, but no way in hell was she going to ask. She'd find out soon enough. "So guess what I was doing when you called."

"You were sitting in court."

"Oh. I already told you."

"No, that's just usually what you do in the mornings anymore."

Nicki smiled. "Oh, that's not good. I'm getting predictable in my old age." Sean nodded, still grinning. "But I think I've finally got a case that might get me on the front page."

"Yeah? What's that?"

"Well, there's this guy who was arrested for arson. I have no idea how the cops figured it out, but apparently he burned some guy's house to the ground."

"The dumbass was probably bragging about it on Facebook to his friends."

"Maybe. But what's weird is the victim's house was in Colorado Springs. So I'm wondering why the cops here even care. Why not let El Paso County deal with it?"

"Isn't it *your* job to find out, investigative reporter?"

CHAPTER THREE

NICKI FINALLY LEFT Sean's garage. She revved her beat-up decade-old red Volkswagen Jetta and heard Korn playing on the radio. The station was playing one of her favorite Korn songs, "Got the Life," so she cranked the radio, then shifted into drive. She had to head over to the newspaper to talk with her editor.

Why had it been so hard to be around Sean today? Why? She knew why. She'd just broken up with her latest "boyfriend" last week and so all her thoughts came back to focus on Sean again, like a lion's intense gaze on the zebra across the plain. Her thoughts always snapped back to Sean when she wasn't distracted by a boyfriend du jour. And sometimes even the boy toys weren't enough.

But this whole Kayla thing had Nicki unnerved. Sean had never been this serious about a girl before. This could be *really* serious.

Which meant that Nicki had to finally find a way to get over him once and for all.

That was easier said than done. They'd become friends in high school while doing theatre together. Sean was the sound guy, while Nicki loved the limelight. So many hours spent together, especially at cast parties and impromptu gatherings, led them to discover that they had a lot in common. They both loved the same music, the same TV shows, the same books (although Sean wouldn't have admitted to his other friends that he liked to read), even the same classes, and they both liked playing paintball and snowboarding. They found themselves spending more and more time together, but they were just friends. Nicki had been dating the same boy all through high school up until he left for college in California anyway, and so she hadn't thought of Sean like that back then.

After graduation, they attended Winchester Community College together. Sean was taking classes for Automotive Science, while Nicki—unsure of what she wanted to do with her life—worked on an Associate of Arts. Her advisor told her she could then transfer to a four-year university and maybe by that time Nicki would figure out what she wanted to do. No such luck. She finished school, all right, but was still clueless about where she wanted to go after that. So she figured she'd take a few years off from school and come back when she had a clue.

Eight years later, she was still clueless.

Sean never finished getting his degree. After a year of classes, especially ones like Basic Algebra, Composition, and Biology, he decided he was done. He figured he knew enough about motorcycles (one of his passions) to open up a repair shop already, and what he didn't know, he could teach himself. The first two years, his mom let him work out of her garage until he'd earned enough money to rent a place of his own. Since then, his business (and reputation) had grown enough that he'd had to move his business one more time for a bigger place.

But it was during that time that something transpired between Nicki and Sean, The Night That Must Never Be Mentioned Again. Easy to avoid talking about, maybe, but Nicki would never forget it.

Her two-year college plan turned out to last three years, and sometime during the first year she'd fallen for a guy she met in one of her classes. Brent was a few years older than she and good looking. They dated for a year and a half, and Nicki had begun to think of him the way she suspected Kayla was now thinking about Sean. Nicki had thought maybe Brent could be the one. She'd been thinking about it for a few months. Her parents liked him, and he had a bright future. He was planning to attend a university in either Denver, Colorado Springs, or Pueblo once he graduated a semester later, and Nicki had begun thinking about following him to whatever school he decided on. That was until the night she'd been on the WCC campus studying for the Abnormal Psych midterm in the library with a group of friends. It was late, probably close to ten, and the work study student manning the desk had warned them that the campus was closing up soon. Nicki excused herself from the group to use the restroom before picking up her books. But the three stalls in the little restroom across the hall from the library were already being used, and she didn't want to wait. So she walked down the hall to the other end of the building. Even though most of the lights were already turned off down there in preparation of closing, she figured security wouldn't care if she used the restroom anyway. The bathrooms on campus had motion-sensor lights, so she knew the lights in there would switch on as soon as she entered. That particular restroom was the biggest one in the building, with seven stalls, including one large handicapped-access one. She wouldn't have to wait in there.

Except the lights were already on, and someone was using the large handicapped stall, and that someone wasn't taking a piss. That someone was getting fucked. So she was in a dilemma—*now that I've prolonged it and I really need to go, do I just go for it or do I go back down the hall and use that one?* She really had to go and, she figured, having people hear your business was a risk the fucking couple should have known they were taking when they decided to copulate in a public place.

She chose the stall next to the door leading outside, so she was several yards away from the large stall at the end of the room. If the couple heard her, she could pretend like she didn't know what was going on. With all the grunting and groaning, maybe someone was just constipated, right? Okay, stupid. So she couldn't play dumb, but her hope was to just pee as quickly as possible and leave before she had to face the horny couple down the way.

There was no way to disguise the steady stream of urine splashing into the bowl. But the couple didn't seem to mind; Nicki could tell because the rhythmic pounding into the metal wall of the stall down the way didn't ease up. Nicki felt embarrassed but smiled just thinking of the story she could tell her study group when they packed up their books for the night. The girl was squealing with delight, and Nicki still didn't register that there was a problem, even when the girl yelled, "Oh, yes, Brent!" Nicki finished up and walked to the sink to wash her hands and that was when she heard the man grunt through gritted teeth, "I'm close, baby." She paused, the water streaming through her fingers, as she realized the man in the stall was *her* Brent. She knew because, for some stupid reason, he'd always felt the need to announce during sex that he was getting ready to ejaculate: "I'm close." She finally managed to swallow the buildup of saliva in her mouth and shut off the water, but she felt as though a robot had taken over her body. In slow motion, she grabbed a paper towel to wipe off her hands and started walking toward the door to the hall. But then she felt an unexpected fury well up inside her and she stomped back to the other side of the bathroom. She pounded on the door to the stall three times and then said, "I hope she squeezes your dick off!" She spun around, heading back to the hallway door, her eyes already clouding with salty tears. As she opened the door and began walking out the hall, she thought she might have heard her name.

And she would never remember exactly what she said to her study mates when she returned to their table in the library; she just knew that she gathered up her belongings and darted out the door before she turned into a blubbery mess, promising to see her peers on test day.

She didn't want to go home; she didn't want to have to talk to her parents about it. And she didn't want to talk to her girlfriends either, who would have told her he was a loser and then would have proceeded to tell Nicki that they'd warned her about what a creep Brent was.

She decided that she wanted to get drunk.

She was legal now, so she had no qualms about it. But she didn't want to drink alone, so she called Sean, her willing partner in crime. He wasn't in bed yet, so he invited her over to his apartment. She promised to bring a twelve-pack.

Brent called her cell phone several times. She never answered and she finally shut it off. When she got to Sean's house, she tried to plaster on a smile, but he asked her what was wrong. Her face must have been streaked with tears. So she told him why she'd been crying. And instead of drinking, he held her close while she sobbed in his arms. After she was able to let the tears go, she continued to rest her head against Sean's chest. "Thank you," she said.

He stroked her hair. "For what?"

"For being here."

"God, of course." They were quiet again for a while until Sean finally said, "Brent's a dumb motherfucker, you know that, don't you?"

"What do you mean?"

"He can't keep his dick in his pants when he's got you. That makes him a dumb motherfucker."

Nicki half laughed, the after-crying-jag endorphins kicking in. "That's so sweet." Smiling, she looked up at Sean, only Sean wasn't smiling back. His mouth was on hers before she could register what was happening. And even though Nicki had relived that night in her mind at least a thousand times since, she couldn't quite remember every detail like she'd wanted to. She remembered his lips on her nipple, causing her to arch her back and sigh. She remembered the easy delectable orgasm she'd had at the touch of his expert fingers. She remembered the swell of his penis as he slid in and out of her and how she had moaned his name as she came again.

Only she hadn't moaned Sean's name. It was that fucker's name, Brent, that had escaped her betraying lips.

She hadn't been thinking about Brent, had in fact been shocked at how awesome Sean was in bed and wondering why the two of them had never done this before. It was like he had The Nicki Handbook and knew exactly how to drive her crazy, knew all the right places to touch her, how to make her melt at his touch, how to just breathe on her to make her come. And she'd never been the same since. She really had meant to say Sean's name but for some stupid-ass reason her mouth had decided to say *Brent*. Un-fucking-believable.

So she'd apologized right after. She couldn't even blame drinking for her gaffe because she'd been stone-cold sober. He said it was fine, that he understood, but she knew better. And when she had to leave a little later (didn't want mom and dad asking where she'd been all night long—that's what happened when you decided to save money by living with the parental units), she knew she'd fucked up their friendship royally.

She left the beer on his table. He might want it later.

So things were stiff and uncomfortable for a while, and there was a silent agreement between the two of them. But they stopped spending time together, stopped calling each other, stopped hanging around. Nicki grew tired of it and she went to Sean's garage at his mom's house in between classes one day. She told him, "Look, Sean, I can't take back what I said, and I'm sorry if I hurt your feelings. But I miss having you as my friend. I can't stand this."

Sean had been adding up some receipts at a desk in a corner. He looked up from the papers. "Can't stand what?"

"We don't hang around together anymore. Can't we just go back to the way we were before?"

And they agreed. And with that handshake, followed by pizza and a beer and nothing else, they had decided without saying a word that they would never again talk about The Night That Must Never Be Mentioned Again. And after several uncomfortable months, they'd finally eased back into the friendship they'd once had. Except that it was never the same for Nicki.

It was far easier getting over Brent.

CHAPTER FOUR

NICKI PARKED HER car in the *Tribune*'s employee parking lot behind the building and walked toward the hulking brick structure. The heat outside was climbing, probably in the mid-nineties by now. She was glad she'd chosen the miniskirt topped with a light white cotton short-sleeve blouse and white sandals that showed off her pink toenails. Her long, light brown hair, though, was starting to feel a little smothering, and she was deciding if she wanted to pull it up in a ponytail or just suffer.

She walked in the backdoor through the press area. Normally loud and unbearable, the press was off for now. It wouldn't get revved up until much later in the day. For now, though, the room was an empty shell, quiet and oppressively hot.

She walked toward the doors that led to the main offices of the paper. Once she opened the doors, she felt the air-conditioned breeze blowing down on her arms. The little hairs on them stood at attention while goose bumps formed. *Oh, yeah...our imitation of the North Pole.* Someday she would remember to bring a sweater. She knew she'd be ready to go back outside again after three or four minutes in the cold air. But she needed to talk to her editor first.

Neal Black was a decent guy, probably in his late thirties, if Nicki's judgment was right. She knew this was his first full-fledged editor job, so she suspected that was why he was sometimes a hard ass. He had full, thick, brown hair and brown eyes, with a medium build. And Nicki suspected he wore contact lenses, because when he looked tired, he blinked a lot. She walked through the back hallway, avoiding the pool of reporters and copy editors to the left, instead heading straight for Neal's office.

She saw through the glass on the door that he was on the phone, but he saw her and waved her in. Like an old-time editor, he had the phone wedged between his ear and shoulder and was shuffling papers around on his desk while talking. Nicki wondered why he didn't utilize the speaker phone feature; his office had a door, so it's not like he would be letting confidential information out. Or, at the very least, he could have used the earpiece instead. It would have been a lot more comfortable than what Neal was doing now.

But she supposed that was what he liked to do. She knew from the times she'd spoken to him on the phone that he didn't like being on it and ended conversations as quickly as possible. Maybe if he used the speaker, he wouldn't feel that way.

She entered the office, careful not to make noise with the door, and sat across from Neal in one of the cushioned chairs that faced his desk. Finally, Neal said in his booming voice, "Yeah. Get on that and call me back." He hung up the phone and gave Nicki a weak smile. "Whatcha got for me, rookie?"

If Neal hadn't been such a likeable guy, she would've been pissed that he called her rookie all the time. In all fairness, though, Neal had given her a chance that a lot of other people never would have. When Nicki approached him one year ago, she was working three different jobs—one as a waitress in a pizzeria, one selling makeup door to door, and another answering phones for a used car lot. Working the three jobs kept her busy and kept the bills paid; they also kept her in shape and she got a lot of makeup on the cheap, but she had no social life. Worse yet, she had no future and the pay wasn't great. She knew she liked writing, had always dreamed of being the next Poet Laureate of Colorado or winning the Nobel Prize for Literature but was squandering those skills on things like sending emails to her faithful makeup customers, jotting down phone messages, and writing down customer orders. Enough was enough. So she made an appointment with Neal and begged him for a writing job. He couldn't do that, he said. She had no experience and no degree. He suggested that she shadow one of his reporters, though, to see if she still liked the job after. So she did. She shadowed Diane Glick, the Features reporter, for two weeks.

Neal had probably thought she would have given up, but instead she was more excited, especially when she saw how bored Diane looked by the job. Nicki watched the woman, all the time wondering why she wasn't having more fun. When Nicki met with Neal again, she told him she was just as excited as ever. And she suspected he could use the help.

"Look," she said, "I'll write for free. You can look over my articles and tell me what I need to do to improve. I just want the chance to do this." She loved that—for the most part—Diane had been her own boss, in charge of organizing her own day. She got to meet new people and share with the community her insights on the goings on of the town. Neal relented and told Nicki she could give a court report once or twice a week, summarizing the various little things that happened. It wasn't long before she realized that he had all that information already, as the court's docket was available online. So she instead began adding more information, a little here and there, to the more interesting stories, facts not included on the docket. He began spending a good hour a week with her, coaching her about how to write a solid news story. If she again heard him say, "Who, what, where, when, how, and why," she thought she'd puke. But she started asking herself those questions as she sat to write her articles, and she finally had her first article published three months ago. Two months ago, Neal said he couldn't keep publishing her work...unless he paid her. So she was now published as a freelance journalist, getting paid by the article, and Neal continued coaching her. Since she'd grown tired of writing articles that wouldn't get published because they weren't what Neal was looking for, she'd started running her big ideas past him before spending the time writing. And because she knew Neal hated the phone, she tried to do that in person at least twice a week.

In Neal's office, Nicki glanced at the lined light green sheet in her steno pad to report what she'd learned but looked up before speaking. "Well, here's what I'm thinking might turn out to be a pretty interesting story: Jason Edwards pleaded not guilty to one count of criminal mischief and four counts of arson. I don't have all the details yet, but I want to follow this one. He's accused of setting fire to a guy's house in Colorado Springs last week." She looked back at her notes. "A guy named Charles Baker. All I know right now is apparently the Baker guy was sleeping with Edwards's brother's ex." Neal nodded. "I want to know how the cops figured it out and why they're accusing Edwards and not his brother." Neal smiled but said nothing. "What? What am I missing?"

"The police have an APB out on Edwards's brother too…a guy by the name of Michael Sterne."

How did Neal already know this stuff? "Sterne?"

"Half brothers."

"Oh." Nicki wrote this new information in her pad. God, sometimes Neal made her feel so stupid. But that's why he was mentoring her, she reminded herself. She was *learning*. "So they suspect Sterne was involved too?"

Neal ran his thick hand through his hair. "Oh, they *know*, I'm sure."

"So is this worth following?"

"Why not? More action than we usually see here in Winchester…even though it didn't happen here." He smiled.

Nicki's brown eyes lit up. *Yes.* "So do you want me to type up the initial information from court this morning?"

"Yep. Email it to me when you're done."

"Will do." She felt giddy. This story had to be *the one*. She stepped into the reporter pool and found the cubicle with the computer and phone that was used by all freelancers. Fortunately, no one was using it right now or else she would have had to use another "official" reporter's cubicle, and that was never pleasant. Those reporters and the girl on wants ad—all six of them, including the sports guy—were territorial. In fact, Nicki was surprised they didn't piss all over their cubicles to drive away offenders like herself, just like dogs in the wild. There were two extra cubicles but only one that was equipped to handle a reporter, and being able to use it was always a crapshoot. Sometimes, Nicki would write her story at home and email it in that way, but the computer here was more powerful and faster than her little notebook.

She booted up the computer and settled in. While the computer warmed up, Nicki texted Sean on her phone: *Its a go!* She hated not putting the apostrophe in, but texting had made her lazy when it came to punctuation. It didn't matter—Sean would know what she meant…if he bothered to read it.

She composed a two-paragraph story, then emailed it to Neal. It had taken her twenty minutes as she picked at it. She tried to catch everything Neal would change before dropping it in the paper. She knew it was his job and he certainly knew better than she, but it was still aggravating having her words changed.

Then she scribbled a few to dos in her steno pad. She wanted to talk to a police officer and she thought she might want to talk to Edwards himself. She could do those things tomorrow and maybe have another article (or two) in the paper this week.

She checked the time and realized she needed to hurry

home, grab a bite to eat, and then get in uniform. Napoli awaited her.

CHAPTER FIVE

NICKI HAD QUIT her job answering phones at Crown Auto Plaza—preowned car hell as far as Nicki had been concerned—one month after Neal had taken her under his wing. If she wanted to attend court hearings, she needed a good chunk of the day to do it. But writing for the paper alone wouldn't pay the bills. She continued waiting tables at Napoli Pizzeria and selling makeup to make ends meet.

Nicki hadn't *minded* working for Crown Auto, but she'd slept with one of the mechanics there a few months before and had regretted it since. Ken had been nice enough but definitely not her type (read: lousy in bed), and he became obsessive after she'd broken it off. She didn't want to hurt his feelings, but he didn't get it when she said she was no longer interested. He kept asking, no matter how many times she said no. So being gone from Crown Auto helped. She blocked his number on her cell phone and that was it. Well, that and he came to her apartment one Saturday after she quit, and Sean had been hanging out with her. Ken probably assumed Sean was her new boyfriend and didn't stay long enough to find out for sure. She could have kissed the *BAMF* on Sean's knuckles for scaring Ken off. Of course, it wouldn't have taken that much for her to kiss his fingers anyway.

Crown Auto might have been history, but she still worked for Napoli five nights a week, Tuesday through Saturday. The tips from Napoli were her most significant source of income. She also ran her little tail off every night of the week, because even slow nights were busy compared to most places—Napoli was a favorite of locals and tourists alike, and the place rarely had an empty table during the week. So she kept in shape without having to work out on a regular basis. And since Nicki had been working there for five years, she was the senior waitress (God, she hated that moniker) and could get whatever hours she wanted. And she met a lot of good-looking guys at her job. That was always a plus.

So she squeezed into her black and red uniform. It wasn't the most attractive, but she did what she could with it. The top was short sleeved with a stiff collar, and the pockets had red piping. The back of the shirt said *Napoli* in script on a diagonal from the waist to just below the underarm. It was a button-up shirt, so Nicki usually wore it so that she could show just a little cleavage. She was only a C cup, but she found that if she kept the shirts snug, her C looked good enough to keep the guy's gaze off her eyes for part of the time (usually when she was writing something down). It didn't hurt that she wore a necklace whose heart pendant nested perfectly atop the swell of her two breasts. Her waist was also small enough that anything larger than C would have looked like too much. The black jeans that went with the uniform had red piping down the sides, so half the time she felt like she was in a high school marching band. But they were mostly black, so they looked pretty cool, and they also hugged her ass, another feature she was proud to display. She wore black sneakers with the ensemble. Over the years she found that athletic shoes were the best—they had more cushioning so her feet didn't ache after an eight-hour shift.

Tuesday nights were the slowest, and she'd only had five tables since she'd arrived. *It had better pick up soon*, she thought, because she'd be getting three more people in the next half hour. But, as always, by the time her help arrived—one waiter, one waitress, and a busboy—the place was buzzing and ready for them all.

A couple of hours into their steady stream of customers, three bikers walked in the door. Would they want to sit at the bar or could she persuade them to sit in her section? She'd always gotten great tips from bikers, so she tried to snag them when she could. Mandy and Brian could barely handle what they had, so she'd be happy to take these guys off their hands. She walked to where they stood, by the sign that asked them to *Please Wait to be Seated*, and said, "Are you hungry or just need a little something to quench your thirst?" She wore a flirtatious smile and waited for them to answer.

The tallest one, a lovely shade of brown with smoldering coal eyes, brown hair, and clean-shaven face, smiled back, his teeth a startling white. "What would you recommend, *señorita?*"

Ooh, she was going to *love* waiting on this table, unless, of course, they only wanted the bar. This hot guy was already playing the game. This was going to be fun. "Me? I'd get a large pie and a pitcher. But that's up to you, of course." She made eye contact with his friends, as well, so they wouldn't feel left out, but she ended with her eyes back on Mr. Tall-Dark-and-Fucking-Hot.

He looked at his comrades. "Well, guys, pizza sound good?"

Both of his companions nodded, apparently the strong but silent type, and Nicki smiled again. She reached to the menu stand at her left and pulled out three menus. "Right this way, please." She could feel their eyes raking over her entire backside and she felt chills. Oh, yeah, she'd get a really nice tip out of this table…providing the kitchen didn't fuck it up for her. She couldn't complain, though—the new head cook was finally getting his shit together, so last weekend was better than it had been in quite some time. Tonight would probably be okay too.

She led them to the last empty seat in her section, a quiet booth near the front. "Hey, could we sit over there instead?"

Shit. The short blonde guy in their group pointed over to an empty table in Mandy's section. Not only would Mandy wind up screwing up so badly that Nicki would have to cover her anyway, but Nicki also wouldn't get the nice tip these guys were certain to leave. But…the customer was always right. "Sure," she said, making sure her smile was as wide as it should be. After they got arranged and she passed around their menus, she said, "Our specials tonight are Fettucine Alfredo with a house salad or the Meatball Grinder with kettle chips. I'd like to point out our appetizers on the first page of the menu and recommend the breadsticks. I promise you you've never had breadsticks like Napoli makes. And we have a variety of beers on tap, including Coors and Michelob. If you'd prefer, we have a number of microbrews as well, featured on the back page."

Hot guy looked up from the menu, teeth gleaming, and asked, "What would you recommend?"

She smiled. "Well, I'd start with the breadsticks with marinara and a house salad. I'd probably either get a pitcher of Coors or a bottle of Fat Tire Amber. And then I'd get a large thick crust pizza. I'd probably get the *Everything but the Kitchen Sink*, which has no fewer than five meats and six veggies."

He looked at his friends who barely nodded their assent and said, "That's what we'll have, then. Make it a pitcher, but I'll take a Fat Tire too."

Nicki winced. She said, "Mandy will be your waitress, but I can put in your order for you."

Hot guy said, "What? You don't want to wait on us?"

Nicki slapped on a large mock sad face. "You're not in my section. I'm sorry."

"Our loss, I guess." He paused. "So what's *your* name, Not-Mandy?"

She smiled again. "It's Nicki. What about you guys?"

"I'm Carlos." He waved his hand across the table to first the blonde guy and second the hairy salt-and-pepper brunette who should have thought about using some Just For Men. "And this is Jake and Eddie."

"Nice to meet you all. Enjoy your meal." She smiled one last time. "Mandy will be with you shortly."

Damn. Well, that's what happened when your section

was close to full. She punched the order into the touch screen for the kitchen, then found Mandy spazzing out making two salads in the server area of the kitchen. How that girl managed to consistently fuck up and/or stress out serving only four tables at a time, Nicki would never know. She kept hoping Mandy would quit one night and walk out, but so far, she'd stuck to it. "Mandy, you have three at table twelve."

Mandy looked up, pausing with the dressing ladle in hand. "Shit. Are you kidding?"

"No, but I already got their order. Do you want me to take their drinks to the table?"

Mandy's brows relaxed. "Could you?"

"Sure." It would give her one last chance to flirt before moving back to her tables chockfull of families, couples, and old people. The bartender was busy as well, taking an order from a customer at the bar, so Nicki poured the pitcher of Coors, then fetched a Fat Tire from the fridge and popped the tab. She placed them on a tray, along with three frosted beer glasses, and walked back to Mandy's table. "Here you go, guys," she said, placing first the bottled beer in front of Carlos. And, my, oh my, he'd removed his leather jacket to reveal a smooth, well-defined bicep with a large skull tattoo delicately painted on it. *Yum.* Then she poured their first beers for them, starting with Jake, then Eddie, and finally Carlos. "Can I get you anything else right now?"

Carlos set his bottle down after taking a sip of beer. His eyes climbed from her waist to her eyes. "Your number."

Sweet Jesus. This guy was smooth and had caused—in a mere second—Nicki's legs to melt into rubber. This guy wasn't local, though, that much she knew, so what the hell would he want with her number? Maybe just to see if she was really interested?

She considered him for a moment. No need to seem overly fucking eager and pathetic. Then she smiled, whipped out her notepad, and scribbled down her name and phone number. She ripped the page out and slapped it on the table next to Carlos's beer bottle. Before removing her hand, she said, "Guard this with your life." She smirked and winked, then turned around and walked to her section, checking to see how each of her tables was doing.

She didn't dare look back. No way could she *dare* look over there—not yet, at least.

As the evening wore on, however, she looked over at their table on occasion and got some smiles. Mandy finally got her ass in gear and brought them their breadsticks. Closing time approached—ten o'clock—and Carlos and his guys were on their third pitcher, long having decimated their pizza. She was down to four of her own tables who were either eating or finishing up, so she stood in the server area at the back of the restaurant, printing out the tickets of her tables that were done.

She felt her phone vibrate against her hip and pulled it out. She didn't recognize the number and wondered who would be calling her this late in the evening. She answered it while tapping on the touch screen in front of her. "Hello?"

"Is this Nicki?" The voice was familiar, but she couldn't place it.

"Yeah."

"This is Carlos. I wondered what you're doing after you

blow this joint tonight."

She smiled. Shit—he didn't waste any time. "That depends."

She could hear his smile through the phone. "On what?"

"On who wants to know." She paused. "And why."

She printed out the first ticket and began tapping on the screen again to pull up the next one. *Had to remember to add two orders of cheesecake to it*...if she could concentrate. Finally, Carlos said, "Well, *I* want to know." His voice dropped a little and it sounded husky, sending shivers up Nicki's spine. "I'm leaving Winchester tomorrow and wondered if you'd want to give me a reason to come back sometime."

Holy fuck. How the hell could she say no to this guy? Well, she couldn't. "I won't be done here till at least ten-thirty..." and maybe longer if Brian and Mandy sucked as usual. "We could meet around eleven maybe. Would that work?"

"How about you meet me at the lounge at the Winchester Inn when you're done?"

She grinned and finished adding the cheesecakes, then made the next ticket print out. "Okay. I'll see you then." And not only did she get Brian and Mandy to hustle so that they were done closing by ten-thirty, a first for those two, but she also ran to her apartment to shower. She didn't shampoo her hair, because she didn't have time to redo it, but she sprayed some perfume in it once she took it out of its ponytail. The rest of her, though, smelled like stale grease and garlic. She *reeked* of Napoli, and the shower was essential. But by the time she was done, she smelled like vanilla. What to wear, though? She eyed her little black dress tucked in the back of the closet, a little too snug and a little too short, but she figured Carlos would think it was just right.

CHAPTER SIX

BEFORE LEAVING HER car, Nicki smeared some hot pink lipstick on her lips. She checked in her mirror, relying on the streetlamp over her car to help her make sure she didn't have any on her teeth. She checked her entire face, then stepped out of the car, tugging on the dress a little so her butt cheeks didn't peek out.

She took a deep breath, then walked toward the hotel entrance. The glass doors slid open as she approached, and she looked around the lobby until she saw the sign on the left pointing toward the lounge. Her three-inch black heels clicked on the tile but there was no one around to notice. A woman stood at the desk, but she was on the phone and didn't look up.

Nicki arrived at the door to the lounge. It was dark inside, but her eyes quickly adjusted. She spotted the bar and saw Carlos, sans his friends, nursing a beer. He was talking with the bartender who seemed to be enjoying a quiet evening. Nicki could see only three other people in the bar.

She approached the stool and Carlos looked over. Was that really a look of shock on his face? "Nicki?"

"Hey."

"You look ravishing." Ravishing? Nice. That was the plan. She slid up onto the stool. "Would you like a drink?"

She thought she might. Let's see...he'd had several beers by this point, so she might want something a little stronger to catch up. She didn't want to drink too much, though, for several reasons. One was she had a lot of work to do tomorrow. Two was she didn't want Carlos to not go for it. She knew if she had too much to drink, he wouldn't touch her. Well, probably, but she didn't want to take the chance. Guys could be funny that way. They wanted you a little loose, but not too loose. "I think so." She looked at the bartender. "What's your specialty?"

He shrugged. "How about a White Russian?"

She nodded. "Sounds great."

She looked over at Carlos who had been studying her collarbone, barely covered by a one-inch black strap. His eyes met hers. "So what do you usually do in this town for fun?"

If she had a dime for every tourist who asked... "Depends on what you like to do. I'm sure you already found the biker bar."

"Bad Boys?"

"Mmm hmmm. In the winter there's skiing farther up the mountains. Hiking's big—we have lots of trails. In the summer, there's rafting, and there are a lot of softball and soccer teams that play for fun. A lot of people like camping and fishing. Oh, we also have the water park."

Carlos smiled again, a mocking look on his face, as the bartender placed Nicki's drink in front of her. "I asked what *you* do for fun." Carlos handed several bills to the bartender.

Nicki sipped her drink. "Ah, specifics." She took another sip. "Well, I don't have as much fun as I'd like to. I work three jobs, so they keep me busy."

"Guess I got lucky that you found time for me."

A lopsided grin crossed her face. "No, you just happened to catch me at quitting time." She placed her hand on his. "But I would have made time for you if your timing hadn't been so impeccable."

He squeezed her hand and smiled, then picked up his beer. He asked her to tell him about her other jobs, but she said she would later. She didn't feel like talking about herself, so she asked what he was doing in Winchester. He told her he was on his way to New Mexico but that he had a friend in Winchester he'd wanted to see on his way through Colorado. Jake and Eddie were old friends from Colorado Springs as well. He mentioned that he was going to New Mexico "on business" but left it at that.

Both of them finished their drinks at the same time, and Nicki knew the awkward moment of truth was nearing. But there was nothing awkward about it. Carlos simply leaned close to Nicki and said, "I have a room here. Would you like to stay a while?"

And by the time the door clicked shut to his second-floor room, he had Nicki in a tight embrace, his tongue dancing in her mouth. *Mmmm*...he was good. His lips were then down on her neck and her collarbone next, as he took his leather jacket off, tossing it onto the chair just past the doorway. Nicki felt her hands moving up the back of Carlos's red t-shirt. His back was nothing but muscle, but she could barely concentrate on it. His hands were on her waist and then her ass, and he picked her up, holding her close, her legs wrapped around his midsection.

He pressed her back up against the wall, and all that was between her flesh and him was a thin pair of lacy black panties. She could feel him growing hard and hot, pressed up against his jeans, and she felt her loins respond in kind. His mouth was back on hers and she finished pulling his shirt up. He started grinding up against her until she let out a weak sigh, her fingernails digging in his back.

He picked her up again, but instead of laying her on the bed, he sat her on the round table next to the chair. With one swoop of his forearm, he slid a thick notebook off the table, probably one of those that listed all the hotel's amenities. He leaned down and his hands held her face. He kissed her again, then brushed her hair back with a hand, exposing her neck. He kissed it, lots of small kisses, down the length of her neck, then to her collarbone. His hands moved to her breasts, reined in by her tight dress. But he found the hard, pointed nipples through the fabric and teased them with his touch, rubbing them in a circular motion with his thumbs. Her fingers wound through his hair. He laid her back on the table, kissing her on the lips again, and then got down on his knees. He kissed inside her thighs while his hands pushed up on the dress at her hips. She felt his thumb on top of her wet panties and he massaged until a guttural moan escaped her lips. He then grabbed the panties on either side and slid them down past her knees. She thought he wasn't going to waste his time—

he knew she was ready and he was too, so he was going to fuck her right here on the table.

Only he didn't stand up. Instead, he placed his thumbs on either side of her labia and spread them apart and then she could feel his breath. His tongue, warm and soft, began stroking her clitoris. Her hands found his head again and coiled around his short hair. "Oh…" His tongue started moving faster, faster as her breathing grew deeper and deeper and then the dam broke. Her legs quivered as deep moans rushed out of her throat. His hands pressed into her thighs as his tongue continued to work its magic.

She was still breathing heavily, a quivering mass on the table, as he stood. He unbuckled his belt and unzipped his jeans, then pulled his wallet out of his back pocket and retrieved a condom. She sat up as he unwrapped the condom and pulled his jeans down past his ass. She pulled down his boxers and found the beast inside. She stroked it until he slid the condom on. Her breath was jagged as he made his way inside her pussy and stood, holding her under her bottom, and fucked her standing up. She wrapped her arms around his neck and kissed under his ear. She moved her lips up to his ear and said, "Harder, Carlos." He grunted in response and she felt another orgasm swell. She moaned again and sensed that he was coming too as he pushed her against the wall again, hammering it home.

He stood there a few moments, still holding Nicki, hot breath against her neck. Then he lifted her and laid her on the bed. He lay next to her and dozed off, his jeans still wrapped around his knees, the condom slowly shriveling.

He'd fucked her hard, all right, and good, but he was almost gentlemanly about it. What made her think of that was half an hour later when he awoke and stripped down to nothing, tossing the used rubber in the trash. "Would you stay the night with me, *mi dulzura?*" he asked.

Either he was confusing her with another girl or muttering more Spanish. It *sounded* Spanish and Carlos didn't seem like a dummy, so she figured it was the latter. She wasn't quite sure what he was saying, but it didn't sound like a word she knew. She nodded, smiling, and asked if she could use the facilities first. She splashed a little water on her face and stripped her clothes off, then curled up next to her temporary Latin lover.

CHAPTER SEVEN

CARLOS HAD ASKED Nicki to stay for room service breakfast the next morning ("Order whatever you want"), but she had overslept and knew she had to get something done for the paper before returning to Napoli. They fucked in the shower before she left, but she did have to skip breakfast. And Carlos confessed that *mi dulzura*, loosely translated, meant something like *my sweet thing* in English, so she didn't have to worry that he was calling her by someone else's name. Not that she could ever hold that against anyone...

"Farewell, *mi dulzura* Nicki, until we meet again." She knew a guy like Carlos would never be back in her little town to rock her world again, but it was sweet of him to imply it just the same.

She got home and dressed, feeling top of the world. Nothing like a good lay to take your mind off everything that mattered. She knew she had to at the very least go to the police station today to get some info on Edwards, enough, she hoped, to be an article's worth.

So she sat in the lobby at the police station, waiting to talk to Detective Nathan Wright. After waiting almost an hour, Detective Wright asked Nicki to come to his office. She showed him her "press" card but he seemed unimpressed.

They sat in his small white plain office, Nicki in a chair next to his desk. The office was cramped. Nicki was glad she'd worn a sundress that came to her knees today, but she was wishing she'd worn a jacket. She dress only had thin straps, so she was braless. Somehow, with a cop, she felt like she was indecent. No doubt the steamy morning sex contributed to her feelings of guilt. Must have been that Lutheran background she'd never quite been able to shake…

"What can I do for you, Ms. Sosebee?" She tried not to cringe (or glare) visibly. The police officer pronounced her name "Soh-suh-bee" like many stupid asses before him instead of the correct pronunciation, "Sohs-bee." Two syllables. It was as dumb as when people said "ath-uh-lete." Puh-lease.

Nicki opened the cover on her steno pad. "Please call me Nicki. I'm writing an article on the Jason Edwards case and wanted to ask some questions."

Wright shook his head. "That case is still under investigation, so there's not much I can tell you."

Nicki's pen wilted in her hand. "Well, what *can* you tell me?"

"He's out on bail as of eight o'clock this morning." Nicki jotted it down. "Anything other than that, you need to talk to the District Attorney's Office."

She felt a sigh escape her lips. She wanted to tell him it would have been nice if he could have told her that *before* making her wait an inordinate amount of time, but the last thing she wanted to do was piss off a policeman. Someday he might be able to give her info, so she needed to keep relations smooth. She jotted a note to talk to the DA in her pad and looked up, catching his eyes on the bare skin above her dress. Maybe she *didn't* regret wearing the dress after all…

After striking out with the DA's office as well, Nicki decided to go cry on Sean's shoulder a little bit. Part of her missed the days when she could call one of her female friends, especially Brandy. But Brandy just got married last month, and Brandy—a goodie two shoes—hadn't lived with Kevin before they got married. So Nicki knew they were probably christening every nook and cranny of their new house. Even if they weren't, Brandy just wasn't as available as she used to be, and when she was, she was *with* Kevin. It just didn't feel right anymore. Maybe after some time passed, things would change. And Jillian was even worse. She loved Jillian, but Jillian had three kids now, all under the age of five. So there was no such thing as conversation with her anymore. They were cute kids, great in fact, but they demanded Mommy's attention, and Nicki couldn't blame them. And the last time she'd visited, she'd said *fuck* more than once and got lectured by both Jillian and her husband Nate. Tense and so not worth it.

So Sean it was. It was bright out. It was only ten-thirty, but Nicki could tell today was probably going to be even hotter than yesterday. She had her windows all the way down in the car, and only the breeze kept her from breaking out into a serious sweat.

Sean's blue truck was parked out front, so she knew he was there, but she hadn't ever known a time, Monday through Friday, that he wasn't there. He would be a boss's dream. She walked in the shop and her eyes had to take a moment to adjust. Finally, she saw Sean's outline standing over a bike. He was holding a small notepad and pencil. The bike looked pretty sweet—it couldn't have been older than a year or two. "Hey, Sean!"

He turned around. "Nicki. How's it going?"

Her eyes were still adjusting to being out of the sun, and as they were, she noticed someone else behind Sean on the other side of the bike. Someone tall…someone named Carlos.

He smiled at her and walked over. "Nicki, *mi dulzura*. What a welcome surprise to see you here. What are you doing in a place like this?" He held out his hands as he got near and she thrust hers out in return. He held one, but the right hand he brought up to his mouth and kissed.

She grinned. "I should ask you the same question."

"I went to leave this morning as planned but my bike had other ideas. I called around and found out that Mr. Ramsey here is the best in town, so here I am." He released her hand. "Your turn."

"Sean just so happens to be a very good friend of mine." She lowered her voice. "Probably my best friend, but don't tell him that. I don't want it to go to his head."

Carlos flashed a white smile. "Well, if it takes your best friend more than a day to fix my bike, it looks like I'm going to be looking for companionship again this evening.

Are you free, *mi dulzura?*"

She was really starting to like the way this guy treated her, calling her sweet in an exotic tongue, drinking her in with his eyes every moment. It made her instantly horny. "I think I can be. It's another night like last night, only Wednesdays are busier. But I'm free after I'm done there. Sometime after eleven."

"What do you say? Are you game?" *Hell, yeah, she was game*, but his cell phone rang. "Excuse me a moment." Carlos walked out of the garage into the hot sun. She checked out his ass. Mmm…nice.

God, she felt giddy again after finally calming down enough this morning to act like a professional. She turned around, hoping she'd managed to wipe the shit-eating grin off her face. Sean looked up from the bike. "You *know* that guy?"

Nicki shrugged her shoulders and walked closer. "Yeah."

Sean squatted, looking at the bike up close. "How'd you meet him?"

"At Napoli."

"How long have you known him?"

Nicki swallowed. Why the third degree? "Since last night." Sean shook his head and jotted something on his pad. Time for Nicki to change the subject. She didn't feel like getting grilled. "So…get this. I wait down at the police station for almost an hour this morning until this fucking detective decides to grace me with his presence. Then, when he finally talks to me, he tells me he can't tell me a damn thing!"

Sean looked up at her. "Don't look at me. You know

44

how I feel about cops."

Nicki nodded. "So he told me I had to talk to the DA to get more info. He did tell me, at least, that Edwards is out on bail. So I went to the DA's office. *They* didn't make me sit around, but they did say I have to talk to the Assistant DA Paul Sanders, and he can't see me until tomorrow. So, maybe a tiny article today that he's out on bail, but maybe I'll have more stuff tomorrow—something for a big story."

"I hope so." Sean was distracted. Fine. Nicki knew better—he had a bike in front of him that needed his full adoration and attention. Nicki was no competition.

"Well, I'm going to see if Neal wants me to write something up on today or not. See you later."

Sean grunted something but was really into the bike. *Jesus,* he could at least say goodbye. What the fuck was his problem? Not hers, and she started to walk back toward the front of the shop. Carlos was just coming in and this time he grabbed her about the waist. He was quiet. "So can I call you later and let you know what's going on?"

She smiled. "You better." Carlos kissed her, a deep, toe-curling kiss, holding her in that tight embrace he'd introduced to her last night.

"Until then, *mi dulzura.*"

CHAPTER EIGHT

LO AND BEHOLD, Nicki *did* get that call. She was at Napoli, and he called after five. So the miracle worker Sean wasn't able to fix Carlos's bike in one day's time? Nicki couldn't muster up any tears about that. "But I do have some bad news, *mi dulzura.*"

"What's that?"

"I checked out of my hotel room this morning. I'm staying with some generous friends. But it's a bit...*crowded* here. I can get another room if you'd like, but I can assure you that you don't want to come over here." His voice sounded guttural. "I want you all to myself."

God, he gave her shivers. "I have my own place." Precisely why she'd gotten rid of roommates four years ago. Apartment walls were thin, especially in your own apartment. She didn't like hearing her roommates having the time of their lives when she was alone, and she didn't like the idea of them overhearing when she told a guy at the top of her lungs to fuck her like there was no tomorrow.

Having her own place was pure freedom and worth every penny of the two extra jobs. "Why don't you meet me there after work?"

He agreed—he *did* have access to a vehicle, thanks to his friends—and she gave him the address. He would be there around eleven and sit tight until she arrived. Luckily, she had Deanna on the floor tonight, and Deanna was a great waitress. She wasn't much on teamwork, but she always managed to pull her own weight. Brian was there too, but his lameness was counterbalanced by Deanna. And, it turned out, he wasn't half-bad tonight anyway. So, in spite of how busy they were, Nicki was able to leave a few minutes before eleven.

She didn't see Carlos leaning against the black truck in front of the building. Nicki didn't pay much attention to the vehicles in front of the building anyway, because she had new neighbors every few months, so why bother to get to know them?

The complex was noisy tonight. It sounded like several of the tenants were playing in the pool on the other side of the building Nicki was in, and they were being loud. Nicki knew some of the older tenants would be calling the cops later if the rowdy bunch didn't settle down. The noise distracted her, though, so she didn't hear Carlos walking behind her. As she inserted the key into the lock in her ground floor apartment, she felt hands slide around her waist, making her gasp with fear at first. But then she realized who it must be, and his lips on her bare neck confirmed it. She unlocked the door, turned the knob, and it creaked open, but she felt paralyzed. She couldn't even turn around. She just bent her neck to give Carlos better exposure as a tiny groan escaped her lips.

His left hand moved from her waist and cupped her right breast, and even through the heavy fabric of her shirt, she felt her nipple harden at his attention. His other hand moved to her waistband, where he began unbuttoning her pants. *What was he doing?* She didn't want him to get into her pants in front of her apartment, but she couldn't ask him to stop. It felt too good. And her outside light was off, so there was no spotlight on the activity. So when his fingers found their way under the snug confines of her panties, she felt her breathing grow heavier, and she just let herself go. Carlos's lips and tongue still ravished her neck. "Come for me, *mi dulzura*." Her right arm dropped the purse in her hands and she lifted it up, winding her fingers through his hair.

"Mmmm," she purred, getting closer.

"That's right." His other hand had unbuttoned the top one on her shirt and had made its way inside, and it was working the same magic on her nipple that the other was doing to her clit. She felt herself coming and grabbed on to the doorjamb, stuffing her mouth onto her forearm to stop herself from waking any neighbors who might be asleep.

She felt a fine sheen of perspiration cross her brow as she caught her breath. Carlos extricated his hand from her pants and picked up her purse. Her legs felt like jelly. "So, this is home?"

Nicki managed a smile and pulled the key out of the lock, reaching inside the doorway and turning on the light. "Yep. *Mi casa es su casa*, right?"

He followed her inside. "*Muy bien*…very good."

She took a deep breath and zipped the pants up, not

bothering with the button. She didn't plan on wearing the uniform for too long. "So, can I get you something to drink?"

He declined and sat on a beige chair in her living room. So after Nicki drank a tall glass of water, she returned the favor and gave Carlos a long, drawn-out blow job where he sat, her uniform still on. Then she insisted on a shower. He joined her and shampooed her hair, and then they made love one more time, in her bed of all places. As Nicki drifted off to sleep, she heard the sounds of the pool party dying down at last.

She awoke the next morning as the sun was starting to fill her room. Carlos was getting out of bed. "Leaving so soon?"

He nodded. "It's after seven. I need to return the truck to my friends, and I promised to spend breakfast with them. And then I need to call your friend after eight and see how much more time he thinks he'll need to fix my bike."

Nicki stretched and sat up, the sheet falling to her waist. "Did he say what the problem is?"

"Mmm...you shouldn't do that," he said, looking at her breasts. "It makes it hard to leave."

Nicki grinned, locking her hands together behind her head, making her breasts more prominent. "Don't you want to say goodbye first?" And so he did...in the language of love. Luckily for Nicki, he was fluent in that tongue.

After he left, she showered and dressed. She planned today to interview Jason Edwards himself. Neal had let her write a little two-paragraph blurb recapping his case and mentioning that Edwards posted bail, but she needed something for today, and talking to both Edwards and the DA's office would look great. She was still irritated that they hadn't talked to her yesterday. Either they were putting her off or they really were busy. *Goddamn,* she couldn't wait until she had more clout with the town. She was certain that if her name was as well-known as their star reporter, *someone* there would have met with her that day. She knew part of that was small-town politics too. It didn't matter that Winchester was no longer a town—it was more like a small city nowadays—the mentality was still small town. So she'd have to wait until the DA's office was good and ready.

She'd written down the address on her steno pad. She knew the street, so she headed across town. It was nine o'clock, not too early and—*thank goodness*—not too hot yet. She'd dressed more conservatively today. First, because she was going to be interviewing an alleged felon, and she didn't need to give him any ideas. Second, because she was going to the DA's office after, and she knew she'd never be taken seriously if she couldn't cover her tits and thighs. So she wore a dark blue pantsuit with a sleeveless white blouse and low white heels. She had her hair pulled into a loose bun and wore two tiny gold post earrings.

When she pulled up to the address, she locked her purse in the car and dropped her car keys in her jacket pocket. The only other things she took were her pad and pen and press card. She took a deep breath. She still didn't feel like a full-fledged reporter yet, but she knew just doing it was the training she needed.

She made sure her stride was confident as she walked up the sidewalk to the door. The lawn was really just a little bit of grass, some green, some yellow, mixed with ragweeds and crabgrass, and there was a big plastic toy car, one that a child could sit in, tilted on its side. There was a gray garden hose with a sprinkler on its end, but Nicki doubted it had been used much. On the other side of the lawn was a child's plastic swimming pool, but dirt covered the bottom. It hadn't been used this summer either.

She reached the door and pressed the doorbell. She heard it ring inside and heard commotion inside. "Goddammit, mom, can you get the door?"

This was going to be pleasant.

The temperature might have only been in the low seventies but Nicki felt the sweat beginning to bead up under her bun and behind her collar. She knew it was her nerves, but she reminded herself she could charm people. She just had to be polite. Surely Edwards wanted to tell his side of the story.

At last, the doorknob turned. The screen door remained closed while an older woman with dark hair streaked with gray opened the inner door. The woman's face was lined and covered in small brown age spots. Nicki thought that—with the cocky little shit of a son who was ordering her around—it was no surprise she wasn't aging gracefully. Nicki recognized her as one of the people sitting at Edwards's arraignment. The woman seemed to evaluate Nicki in the swoop of her eyes. Girls like Nicki didn't grace her doorstep every day. When she didn't speak, Nicki said, "Hi. I'm reporter Nicki Sosebee with the *Winchester Tribune*, and I'd like to interview Jason Edwards if that's possible."

The woman drew in a breath, ready to speak, but was interrupted by none other than Edwards himself. He had grasped the edge of the wooden door, just his presence making his mother move over. His face got close to the screen. *Shit.* He was even better looking up close. And, God, he had a pierced eyebrow too, something Nicki hadn't seen in court on Tuesday. But—good-looking or not—he was more trouble than he'd ever be worth to any girl, Nicki could tell just from the temper causing his face to turn red. "What the fuck do you want to know?"

Nicki drew in a deep breath. She hadn't expected him to be so…violent. But what did she expect from someone accused of arson? She forced her sweetest smile. "I just wondered if you wanted to tell your side of the story."

"What story? The one where they're saying I set fire to that house?"

She nodded and looked down at her notes. "Yes. They've charged you with four counts of arson and one count of criminal mischief. But you're innocent until proven guilty. So my job is to provide readers with both sides of the story."

Edwards grabbed his crotch, a silver skull ring on his middle finger glinting in the sunlight that fell in the doorway, and said, "You can tell your readers to suck it."

That was it. If he wanted to be rude, she could be rude back. Nicki held her pen to her pad and asked, "Can I quote you?"

She stepped back when Edwards threw the screen door open, and it barely missed clipping her. "You think that's funny?"

She continued backing up when she heard a voice in the

doorway. "Hey, man, she's cool. Back off."

"She's a *puta*, Carlos. I don't need this kind of trouble."

Carlos stepped out of the house, placing his hand on Edwards's shoulder, stopping the volatile man's progress. "She's cool. I know her." Edwards looked at Carlos, a sneer on the younger man's face. "She's just doing her job." At last, Carlos made eye contact with Nicki. She could see the questions in his eyes, but she knew there was no way he going to let Edwards harm her. She was grateful for that. Carlos said, "If you don't want to answer any questions, you can tell her that. But do you really think it will help your case any if you harass this poor woman?"

Edwards rolled his eyes. "What-the-fuck-ever." He looked over at Nicki and flipped her off with both hands. She'd never been looked at with that much contempt before. The sneer on his face reappeared as he said, "No comment." He turned around, Carlos's hand dropping from his shoulder as he walked back to the house. "Bitch."

Great. So now she was a bitch in multiple languages. And that was after being called sweet in Spanish just earlier that morning. How things changed.

Carlos turned around, watching Edwards reenter the house. He walked closer to Nicki, a small smile on his face, wrapping a protective arm around her shoulder. "So, I take it this is one of your other jobs?"

CHAPTER NINE

THERE WAS NO question in Nicki's mind: Edwards was guilty as hell. Too bad she had to be balanced and fair in her reporting. She'd love to tell the fair citizens of Winchester exactly what she thought about the man.

She knew she'd been lucky Carlos was there. So apparently Edwards's family were the friends Carlos had in Winchester. Carlos rushed her out of there, but not without giving her one last kiss at her car. He said he liked her outfit as he shut her door, then walked to the sidewalk again, waving her off.

What was Carlos's connection to Edwards? Did it matter? She looked at her car clock as she drove away. She still had over an hour before her appointment with the Assistant DA. She didn't want to just sit in their lobby waiting for an hour, so she decided to get a coffee at the Winchester Café and read the Colorado Springs paper, the *Gazette*.

She ordered a venti caramel macchiato and found the

paper. She sat in a corner, away from the glare of the sun. She wanted to see if the Springs' paper had anything about the Edwards case. She spent half an hour browsing through the paper and found nothing. She wasn't surprised, though. Edwards was back in Winchester County, and Colorado Springs had enough of its own crime and misery than to follow the story here. Besides, nothing had really happened yet: Edwards had pleaded not guilty and was out on bail. To a big paper like the *Gazette*, it was no big deal.

She felt wired leaving the café. *Should've ordered the grande instead.* The sugar and caffeine had her hyped up, but it was just as well. She'd been feeling tired before the coffee. That darned Carlos keeping her up most of the night.

She grinned. She'd do it again if given the choice.

She arrived at the District Attorney's office ten minutes early and told the receptionist that she had an appointment with Paul Sanders. The receptionist asked her to have a seat and she picked up her phone.

Nicki turned around, taking in the lobby. It wasn't much to look at—beige carpet, off-white vinyl chairs, and a wooden coffee table that looked out of place. There were several magazines on it, but she didn't feel like reading. She reviewed her notes and the questions she'd written and felt prepared when Assistant DA Sanders opened the door. "Ms. Sosebee?" She stood, smiling and extending her hand. Sanders managed a weak smile in return but did give her a firm handshake. "Follow me."

As Nicki followed Sanders down the hall, she was pleased to notice that the employee area was better cared for than the lobby. Sanders's office was plain—off-white walls, mahogany desk, three chairs, and a well-stocked bookshelf along one wall—but functional...and neat. He had a desk calendar, a pen, and two file folders on his desk, along with a phone and PC. That was it. And everything was aligned in square angles—there was nothing just strewn on his desk; everything had been purposefully placed.

So this guy was anal.

That told Nicki to be to the point...no chit-chat, no niceties. She thought she could manage. Sanders said, "So you have some questions about the Edwards case, is that right?"

She nodded. "Yes. Detective Wright told me I'd have to speak with your office about the case."

His lips pursed together. Sanders seemed to be a humorless sort of guy. Nicki guessed this because he had a severe line between his eyebrows but no laugh lines by his lips. His brown hair was thinning and almost nonexistent on top of his head, and he wore round wire-rimmed glasses. "Well, as you know, we have charged him with one count of criminal mischief and four counts of first-degree arson." She nodded. "What else would you like to know?" He paused. "Have you seen the arrest affidavit?"

She paused, forcing herself to keep her mouth closed. *Arrest affidavit?* And why hadn't the kind Detective Wright offered that to her? Asshole. She finally spoke. "No, I haven't seen it."

"I can get you a copy. It would probably answer any questions you might have." She nodded. *Yep. It might.* He stood. "I'll have the secretary make a copy for you. You can still call if you have other questions after reading it." He handed her his business card.

She felt so stupid. Sean was going to love hearing about how the cop fucked her over. She probably could have had a great story yesterday if she'd known… The good news? This would never happen to her again. She guessed Neal was right: she *was* a rookie, and everyone knew it.

Sanders walked her back out to the lobby. He handed the receptionist a file. "Marla, can you please make copies of the arrest affidavit for Ms. Sosebee?"

She nodded, then took the file and turned around to the copy machine behind her. Sanders said, "Nice to meet you," then let the door shut between them.

Nicki stood by the desk and waited while Marla flipped through the file and then copied two sheets of paper. She turned around and handed them to Nicki. "Thanks," she said and walked out the door. Now she had a lot of work to do.

She decided to work at home on her laptop. She got home and changed into a pink tank top and short white shorts and made a peanut butter and strawberry jelly sandwich. Then she sat down and pored through the papers in front of her. She could see the story unfold in front of her eyes. She turned on the laptop, first finding Slipknot's *Iowa* CD in the media player and cranking it. She wrote best to Slipknot, and she needed a great story today. So she decided to present what the arrest affidavit told her: She summed up that charges were filed against Edwards (something anyone who'd been reading the paper would know by now), and then she began to nail down the facts of the case thus far. Edwards was the younger half-brother of Michael Sterne, also charged in the case, who had—thus far—eluded capture. As Neal had told Nicki a couple of days ago, the police had an APB out for Sterne's arrest, but he was not yet in custody.

According to the arrest affidavit, one Charles Baker of Colorado Springs had fires set to his home two months earlier, and those fires destroyed the house. Charles Baker was dating Sterne's ex-girlfriend, Melissa Jacobs, the month prior to the fires. The arrest affidavit went on to state that Sterne's cell phone was pinging off towers in Winchester County on April thirteenth, the day and time of the fires, and Edwards's phone was pinging off towers in Colorado Springs in return. There were also multiple calls made between the two men during the time of the fires. In March, Sterne had been arrested already with an assault charge. Baker had been visiting Jacobs in Winchester at the time and Sterne had gotten in Baker's face over it.

So now Nicki knew how the police had figured it out, but she still didn't understand why the men were being charged in Winchester instead of in Colorado Springs. She found Paul Sanders's business card and dialed it on her cell phone. She knew she'd wind up getting the secretary, but maybe he would call her back right away since he'd offered to answer further questions.

"Assistant DA Sanders." Well, *hello*. She had his direct line. This could come in handy.

She smiled. "Hi, Mr. Sanders. This is Nicki Sosebee. I've gone over Jason Edwards's arrest affidavit, and I do have one question."

"Shoot." Maybe not as humorless as she'd originally imagined. She was glad to hear that.

"Why are Edwards and his half-brother being charged in Winchester instead of El Paso County?" She cleared her throat. "This is on the record, by the way."

She could hear a smile in Sanders's voice. "I assumed so." He paused. "Edwards and Sterne are being charged here because Sterne was first arrested when he assaulted Charles Baker. That criminal activity occurred in Winchester County, not El Paso. And, further, the two men planned the arson here in Winchester County as well."

Nicki jotted his information down. "How do you know they planned the arson here?"

Sanders didn't answer at first. "I'm not at liberty to say."

Didn't matter—he'd already said it...*on the record*...so she would quote it. She didn't have to say *how* they knew.

"Is there anything else you think I should know?"

"No, I don't think so. Those are the questions I would've asked in your shoes."

Nicki hoped that Sanders would turn out to be a solid contact in the DA's office. Even if not, he'd been of immense help today. She finished writing out her story, including at the end that Sanders had refused to comment. She then pounded out a first paragraph that told—in true journalist fashion—the most important but bare-boned facts of the story, and then emailed it to Neal. She followed up with a phone call, letting him know the story was on the way.

And she still had two hours before she had to go to Napoli, so she decided to go brag to Sean about her killer story.

CHAPTER TEN

NICKI'S CELL PHONE rang just as she was grabbing her purse and heading toward the door. Even though she hadn't programmed the number into her phone (yet), she recognized the number as Carlos's. She was curious and paused inside the doorway to answer it. "Hello?"

"Ah, Nicki, *mi dulzura*. I wanted to tell you goodbye."

"Are you leaving Winchester now?"

"Yes. I'm already a day behind, but thanks to your friend, I can leave today." He paused. "I plan to call you next time I'm in town."

Nicki smiled. "I'd expect nothing less." She inhaled. "Maybe I can catch up on my sleep before you come back."

She heard him laugh. "I'm in trouble then, because if what we did last night was you tired, I won't be able to handle you well rested, *chica*."

She giggled. "You know what I mean."

"I do." She heard the rev of a motorcycle. "Take care of yourself."

"You too, Carlos." She hung up the phone, feeling sadder than she would have expected. Of course, Carlos was meant to be one night only and he'd wound up performing an intense encore. Ah, well, he'd been enough fun to take her mind off Sean for a while, and maybe that would be enough to tide her over until she found her next boyfriend. But the poor suckers who played her BFs never stood a chance.

She arrived at Sean's garage, glad that she'd changed out of the hot suit. It was blazing out again, and even though it was about ten degrees cooler in Sean's garage, it was still *fucking hot.* Sean had Godsmack blaring out of the stereo, so she knew he was in full-on work mode.

She saw him working on a bike in the back of the shop and *goddamn.* The boy had his shirt off. How the *fuck* could she maintain eye contact and have a normal conversation with him if he had his shirt off? As she got closer, she saw that he had a tattoo on his lower back that she'd never seen before. She couldn't tell what it was and wouldn't have a chance, because he stood and turned around just as she got closer.

And the sight of his naked chest took her breath away. He was pure, sweet man, through and through, the ideal for Nicki. Sean might have only been four inches taller than Nicki, but height didn't make the man. Solid, lean muscle, lovingly cared for, with just a little bit of hair on the chest, dark brown nipples, and a six-pack. Mmmm. That was the ticket. And to think she'd actually caressed that hunk of man there before. But she'd blown it eight long years ago. And she was about to make a total fucking ass of herself now if she couldn't concentrate. So she forced her silly licentious grin to become a friendly, warm smile. It was one of the hardest things she'd had to do in a while. "Well, you sure impressed the shit out of Carlos today."

"He should be." Why did Sean look so...*pissed?* He walked over to the stereo and turned the music down. Probably a good idea, since "Re-Align" was ending and the next song, "I Fucking Hate You," wouldn't make the rest of the businesses on the block very happy. As he turned back around, Nicki noticed it for the first time—his bike...his *obsession*...was gone.

"What the fuck, Sean? Where's your bike?"

A puff of air escaped his open lips. "Why do you think Carlos is so goddamned impressed?"

Nicki felt her eyes widen. "You *gave* him your bike?"

Sean gritted his teeth. "No. I sold it to him."

"Why the hell did you do that?"

Sean turned around, walking back to the bike he'd been working on when she'd come in. "He was in a hurry."

Nicki thought of Carlos holding her in front of her door last night bringing her to sweet orgasm and forced back a grin. "He wasn't in *that* big a hurry. Trust me—I would know."

"That's what you think." He picked up a wrench from off the bench beside the bike. "This is his bike here, and it's got a fucked up tranny. I had too many other things to do, so I couldn't get his bike fixed as fast as he wanted." He paused. "But he paid me my asking price for my bike, so I guess I shouldn't complain."

Sean knelt over again and began loosening a bolt on the bike, his back to her again. Nicki's eyes started to drift to the new tattoo just above his waistband when it hit her.

Sean *wanted* Carlos gone. That was the only explanation she could find. She stormed over to stand on the other side of the bike. "No, Sean, that's what you *want* me to think. But *you* wanted him out of here."

He stopped working the wrench but he didn't look up. "What the hell makes you think that?"

"You just decided—as a supposed 'convenience'—to let Carlos buy the bike you've been working on for three years?"

Sean stood, dropping the wrench back on the bench. He looked angry. He was wiping his hands on a rag and then his eyes locked on hers. "What the fuck are you doing hanging with that guy, Nicki?"

She felt her blood grow warm. "What's wrong with him?"

Sean walked around the bike and got closer. "Jesus. Seriously? He's in a *gang*, Nicki, a big one out of New Mexico. Do you really want to be involved in that kind of thing?"

She huffed. "He didn't *act* like a gang member."

Sean smiled and shook his head as he continued closing the gap between them. "What exactly does a gang member act like?"

She took a deep breath. He was getting too close, too close for her to concentrate. She could smell him…Sean always smelled like sandalwood and—well, Sean—and he was more potent today than usual. Maybe it was the thin sheen of sweat on his chest that also made his pecs look so fucking gorgeous? She gulped. *Shit*. She had no idea what to say. "Not like Carlos." Sean chuckled, stopping about a foot away from her. Enough at least so that Nicki could get her bearings. "Why do you care anyway?"

His eyes stayed on hers. "Because you're my friend, Nicki, and I know what these guys do." Then his eyes dropped to her lips.

She intended to call his bluff.

"Bullshit. You wouldn't just give your bike away for that. You know I can take care of myself."

His voice was low. "You're right." His eyes locked on hers again as he placed his hands on both sides of her face, drawing her into a kiss. Nicki thought her heart had stopped beating until she felt it thudding against her chest, as though she were a rabbit being chased by a fox. Her hands cupped his pecs, and she felt the damp warm sweat, felt the hard muscle respond to her hands. Tasting Sean and smelling him up close made the effects of the venti caramel macchiato this morning seem like drinking mother's milk. God, he tasted good.

The kiss ended and Sean pulled back. Nicki's eyes stayed closed, her hands now touching only air. She couldn't catch her breath, and she didn't want the moment to end. She heard Sean say, "Shit. That didn't happen."

Nicki's eyes popped open. She was speechless. "Uh, yeah, I think it did." She had a pair of dripping wet panties to prove it.

Sean's face was stone. "No, it didn't."

Nicki's tongue played with a molar on the left side of her mouth. She was getting ready to speak, trying to think up a good retort, when she heard a *click click* at the other end of the garage. Sean looked in Nicki's eyes again, sending her some coded message, something she couldn't quite register, and then his eyes darted back to his visitor.

That's when Nicki figured it out.

She turned around for confirmation and saw Kayla, wearing tight jeans and a yellow halter top, her tiny B-cup failing to fill its form. Kayla's long red hair bounced as she clicked toward Sean, extending a brown paper bag. "Lunch."

Sean smiled at her. "Thanks, babe."

Nicki tried not to puke. Sean's arms wrapped around Kayla's waist as Kayla's arms wound around his neck. Nicki saw Kayla's white thong string above her jeans, accenting her tramp stamp. God, Kayla was such a stereotype. Nicki couldn't figure out what Sean saw in the girl. But she was nice enough, more than she could say about some of the women Sean had dated in the past. Kayla turned around, long enough that Nicki had wiped the disgusted look off her face. "Hi, Nicki."

"Hey, Kayla. How've you been?" *Did you taste my lips on your boyfriend?* Oh, that was cruel, even for Nicki. Thank goodness she didn't say it out loud. Nicki made sure to leave just as Sean was biting into the sandwich. There was no way they could resume their conversation now. It would just have to wait.

CHAPTER ELEVEN

NICKI WAS SCRATCHING her head, trying to wake up to the phone ringing. It was Friday, one of two days she tried to sleep late on purpose, because she had to work until midnight or later on Friday nights. But leave it to mom to not pay attention to the time of day or day of the week when calling her daughter or even remember that Nicki worked nights. When she saw her mom's number on her cell phone, she thought some of ignoring it. But then she'd get the two-minute message followed by "Call me." It was better to just deal with it now.

Nicki's voice sounded like Selma and Patty, Marge Simpson's sisters, until she cleared her throat. "Hi, mom."

"Hi, honey." There was a pause. "Are you not feeling well?"

Nicki shook her head, a gesture her mother couldn't appreciate. "No, mom, I just woke up."

"Oh, for heaven's sake, Nicki."

"Mother, I didn't get home from work until after eleven. And then I was up till after midnight because I was so wound up from closing the restaurant." She pinched the bridge of her nose between her eyes. "What time is it anyway?"

"Nine."

Christ. She couldn't exactly chew her mom's ass, no matter how tempting. "So, anyway, mom, what's up?" Might as well get her to the point. Maybe Nicki could grab another hour (or five) of sleep if mom could wind it down quickly.

"Well, Will is coming home tomorrow, and we're having dinner Sunday afternoon. Can you make it?"

Will was Nicki's younger brother. He was more intelligent, more driven, and more on the ball than Nicki had ever dreamed of being. And she loved him dearly. "Of course. What time?"

"Two sound okay? I'll probably make pot roast, mashed potatoes, green beans, and maybe lemon bars for dessert."

"No problem, mom. You had me at Will." She missed him more than she'd ever thought she would have, but that's because Will had been going to school *forever*. He went off to college right before he turned nineteen. Since then, he'd graduated from two schools, one with a bachelor's degree, the other with a master's. He was still at the school he'd earned his master's degree from, now working on his doctorate. He was majoring in economics. He had just started working on the PhD last fall, but Nicki thought—even once he could graduate—Will would never live close by Winchester again. With all those smarts (and student loans to pay back), he'd certainly find a killer job teaching at some Ivy League university. So anytime he was back home, she wanted to spend some quality time with him.

Nicki felt herself dangerously close to waking up entirely. "Do I need to bring anything?"

"Just yourself, dear."

"Okay, mom. Thanks."

"By the way, dad and I are proud of you."

Here we go. The comparisons of the disappointing child with the dream kid. What the hell did mom plan to say? Nicki tried to stifle her irritation. "For what?"

"For your newspaper article, of course. Great job, honey."

God, what a shit she was, ready to pounce on her mother. Nicki needed to remember that sometimes parents were actually cool and sincere. "Thanks, mom. There's more where that came from." That was it, though. She was awake now. "Where was it?"

Her mom laughed. "In the paper, of course. You know I don't read the online edition."

Nicki smiled. "No, mom. Where in the paper?"

There was a pause. "Oh. It was on the front page."

Nicki squealed. "On the fucking front page? Yahoo!" Her elation died down to dread in less than two seconds.

"Nicole Lee Sosebee! Watch your language."

Shit. It sucked being a fucking sailor mouth when your parents were hardcore Lutherans, convinced that one of the steps to heaven included a mouth so clean, Saint Peter could eat out of it. Thinking of Will and her mom and dad, Nicki was convinced she was adopted. That was the only logical explanation.

So much for getting more sleep. As soon as her mother hung up the phone, she darted out the door for her copy of the paper. She didn't think about the fact that she was just wearing a clingy t-shirt and panties when she walked out the door. She doubted anyone saw her, and if they did, they probably also saw her little tryst with Carlos earlier in the week and had begun scoping out Nicki's doorway for the next free show. Better than Cinemax.

She kicked the door closed with her foot, pulling off the red rubber band tied around the paper. She saw it, though, before she even finished unrolling it: "Suspect charged in arson case." Neal usually wrote the headlines, although he was open to suggestions. He'd never taken one of Nicki's, so she hadn't offered in a while.

Nicki's eyes continued devouring the paper. Just underneath the title was her first real byline: Nicki Sosebee. Yes! Finally. All her hard work and attention to Neal's guidance was beginning to pay off.

Well, maybe not so much, she thought as she scanned the article. Wow. He'd really butchered her words, especially the third paragraph. By the time she was done reading it, her balloon had deflated. She didn't recognize parts of it at all. But, then, she reread the first paragraph again. And again. And again. Then she smiled. Neal hadn't changed a single word in her first paragraph…the six reporter questions paragraph. Maybe she *was* learning.

The smile was back on her face, and she picked her cell phone back up off the kitchen table. She'd almost finished speed dialing Sean when she pressed *End*. No fucking way was she going to call. No way. There was no way in hell she was just going to pretend like that kiss yesterday hadn't happened. And if she called him right now to celebrate her first front page article (goal accomplished!), that's what she'd be doing—giving him permission to make believe things were still the same.

And maybe they were, but they were going to talk about it first and agree on it.

Where the hell had that kiss come from? He'd never so much as laid a hand on her in anything but a platonic fashion since Nicki's royal fuck up on The Night That Must Never Be Mentioned Again. In fact, he'd treated her more brotherly than Will ever had. He'd made it clear that if they were to have a relationship, friends were all they ever would be.

It was a game of pretend.

And apparently that's what Sean wanted. But they weren't just going to fall back into friendship, not this time, not without talking about it. Nicki might have made the worst mistake in bed ever (worthy of being number one on a David Letterman Top Ten list), but Sean crossed the line he'd drawn in the sand eight years ago, and now he was going to have to be a man and talk about it.

CHAPTER TWELVE

NICKI WASN'T READY to talk about the kiss, no matter how she felt. It was too fresh, and she knew that if she confronted Sean today, she'd blather on and on like a pathetic school girl. If it was just some freak of nature thing that had happened and she wound up confessing her undying—*whatever*—to Sean, he'd cut off their friendship entirely, like he almost did after The Night That Must Never Be Mentioned Again. Nicki just knew it. So she needed a day or so to steel herself, and then she'd be ready to talk. Calmly. Rationally. Like a man.

She didn't get anything done for the paper that day. It's not that she didn't have plenty of time. Between her mother's phone call and agonizing over Sean, though, she was worthless. In that sense, she was glad she didn't have a nine-to-five with the *Tribune*.

But she couldn't stand it anymore. Who to call? Brandy or Jillian? The newly wedded lovebird who would likely see everything through rose-colored lenses with Gucci frames or the frazzled mother of three who would only hear half of what she said thanks to screaming kids in the background trying to light the house aflame but who would offer some great advice?

She started pulling up Brandy's number on her cell phone and began imagining the start of their conversation: "Oh, hi, Nicki. So glad you called. Yes, Kevin and I have had sex every single night since we got married, some nights as many as three times. Yes, I orgasm every time, sometimes experiencing multiple orgasms. He holds me close until I go to sleep. He brushes my hair. He gives me killer backrubs. So...Sean who? Oh, Nicki. Time to move on, don't you think?"

Uh, yeah. Well, maybe not. Jillian's kids might block out a good three-fourths of what Nicki had to say, but Jillian would be able to read her facial expressions. She would be able to empathize, even if she couldn't give Nicki any advice. And, really, that was all she needed.

So she instead dialed Jillian's number. It rang one, two, three times. *C'mon, Jillian, pick up.* Nicki was ready to hang up when, at last, she heard a frantic Jillian on the other end.

"Thank God you answered the phone. I need some serious girl time."

"That sounds fantastic. I have one little boy I could take shopping with me, and—for your girl time—you can babysit these two little girls before I pull my hair out."

Maybe today was a bad day. "Ooh, sorry to hear that."

"Why didn't you tell me to say no to Nate when he proposed?"

Nicki smiled. "Because, Jill, that's not what friends do. You'd be living with me now, laying on my couch, eating

Ben and Jerry's, and only bathing when I forced you to."

Jillian snickered. "That's pretty much what I do now. Nathan, stop playing in the water!"

Nicki winced as Jillian yelled in her ear. "Ouch."

"Oh. Sorry about that. So when do you wanna come over?"

"Well, I have to be to work at four, so how about now?"

"Sounds great. I'll save some macaroni and cheese and apple juice for you." *Oh, would you please?* "By the way, nice front page, girl. You're movin' up."

Nicki felt better already. "Thanks, girlfriend. See you in a bit."

She was glad she'd worn shorts and a t-shirt, because just inside the yard she got sprayed with the hose. "Thanks, Nathan." The little bugger giggled and ran around the back. Good thing. Nicki was stronger than the little shit and would have no qualms about holding the hose down his shirt until it puffed up, full of water. Then again, spraying the hose in his face might get his attention better.

Good thing she wasn't a mom.

She got to the screen door and shouted inside. Apparently, Jillian wasn't running her cooler and was instead letting the breeze through the windows. Newsflash. Ninety-five degree breezes will *not* cool the house down, no matter what the wind speed. Well, she supposed Jillian had to be able to hear the kids when they were outside. "Hey, Jillian, it's me." She started to open the door when shfffft! Nathan blasted her on the side of the head, then ran to the side of the house again, the hose following him around the corner, giving away his position. If she'd had more energy, she would have considered running around the other side of the house and really getting him.

Shit. Good thing she would have to pull her hair back for work. The entire side of her head was dripping. She opened the door and darted inside, no longer caring if she dripped on Jillian's carpet. She had to escape the little monster named Nathan. "Jillian, I'm here!"

She heard a baby crying near the back of the house. "I'm back here changing the baby's diaper. I'll be out in a minute."

The three-year-old Anni toddled out, holding a sippy cup in one hand and animal crackers in another. Nicki leaned over. "Hey, sweetie. How have you been?"

Anni grinned at her, placing her cup in her mouth and tipping it. Then she held out her other hand to Nicki. "For you." Nicki managed a nervous smile and held out her hand. The child placed a sticky, soggy cookie in her palm, smiled again, and then waddled off in the direction she came from. Nicki shuddered and spied a box of facial tissue next to the couch. It was empty. She sighed, trying to be as stoic as possible, heading to the kitchen and trying not to freak out as the cookie attempted to dissolve its way into her hand. God, she was *never* going to have kids. Jillian's children convinced her that it was the shittiest fucking idea ever. Thank the stars for birth control.

"Hey, where'd ya go?"

"I'm in here, in the kitchen washing my hands. Anni nailed me with some god-awful apple juice-animal cracker-cooties concoction."

Jillian rounded the bend to the kitchen, laughing. Her short black hair wasn't styled but looked natural and pretty, and her green eyes sparkled as she approached her friend. "Think of it as an immunization."

Nicki forced a half smile. She looked down at baby Grace. "What have *you* got in store for me, you little booger?"

"She had quite a stink bomb for you, but I cleaned her up before you got here. Next time I can save it."

Be good, Nicki. "Gosh, thanks." Wow—she managed to control that potty mouth. She'd have to do something nice for herself later.

In spite of remembering why she was no longer a frequent visitor at her friend's house, once the kids calmed down, Nicki remembered why Jillian had always been such a good friend. She was a great listener and she helped Nicki think things through. And so she decided to tell Jillian about the entire week. She started just jumping straight for the kiss from Sean and then thought maybe her friend needed to hear about how they got there, so she backtracked to first meeting Carlos and the adventures that ensued (sans the exhibitionist orgasm on the ground floor of her apartment building).

Jillian said, "Hold that thought." She ran in the living room, turned on the television, and started flipping through channels faster than a fuel-injected stockcar at the Indy 500. "Hey, kids, I put SpongeBob on TV." Of course. Wouldn't want to give the kids any ideas.

She came back into the kitchen. "Do you want a glass of iced tea?"

"No, thanks," Nicki managed, not wanting to tell her that she was grossed out by even thinking of consuming anything in her house, especially after the animal cracker paste. God knows what the kids did to anything there.

Jillian sat back down at the table and her voice dropped. "So, Nicki, you're still having one-night stands? What's up with that?"

"Carlos wasn't a one-night stand."

"Okay. Let's nitpick. A two-night stand is so much better."

Nicki stammered. "Well, yeah, it is. You get to know each other better."

"Oh, come on, Nicki. You're going to be thirty this year. Shouldn't you—"

"Jesus, Jillian, I did *not* come over here to get lectured."

Jillian sighed. "Sorry. I just worry about you."

Nicki shrugged. "Fine." She paused. "I forgive you for that. But I can't forgive you bringing up my age."

Jillian laughed. "You're too much." Her eyes darted to the living room to make sure the kids were properly enrapt, then turned back to Nicki. "So, anyway, tell me the rest of the story."

Nicki took a deep breath. "Well, crap. I don't know if I should now."

"Ah, come on. I worry about you, but I trust you. I just feel like it's my duty as a responsible friend to let you know I care." Nicki stuck her tongue out at her. "Now where the heck is this going?"

"Well, the next day, Carlos left. I didn't think anything of it, figuring Sean the master motorcycle mechanic got his bike back on the road without a hitch. But later that day I went by his garage. Do you remember that bike that was his pride and joy?"

"You mean the one he hardly drives but is always

customizing?"

"Yeah, that one." Jillian nodded. "Well, when I went over there, I noticed it was gone. So I asked him about it. And get this…he told me he sold it to Carlos because Carlos was in a big…effing hurry to get out of here." Nicki saw Jillian was intent on her every word. "But believe me when I tell you that was *so* not true. He was enjoying the excuse to spend more time with me."

"You sure?"

"Yeah, I'm sure." She lowered her voice, even though she could hear SpongeBob's giddy staccato laughter floating into the kitchen. "We said goodbye after the first night, because he was going to leave town. I figured that was the end of it. But he made a point of telling me he wanted to get together again since he was stuck in Winchester. I'm not saying it's love or anything even resembling it, but we were…compatible, and he wanted to take advantage of that."

"Okay. So then what?"

"So Sean was lying to me about selling it to Carlos because Carlos was supposedly in a big effing hurry. And so I grew a pair and confronted him about it."

Jillian leaned over the table, getting closer to Nicki. "What did you say?"

"I said something like, 'No, Carlos didn't want to leave. *You* wanted Carlos to leave'."

"Are you freaking kidding me? So what did he say to that?"

"Oh, a bunch of bullshit. Oh, sorry." Jillian waved halfheartedly toward the living room—obviously, the kids were engrossed with *SpongeBob SquarePants* and wouldn't notice Nicki's outburst. "He asked why I was hanging out with Carlos, saying that Carlos was a gang member."

"Seriously?"

"I don't know if it's actually true or not, and it doesn't matter."

"Yeah, I think it does. That could be dangerous."

Nicki sighed. "Carlos was really sweet. And gentle. And a gentleman. If all gang members were like he was, the world would be a better place."

Jillian grinned and rolled her eyes. Her voice was strained, rising in pitch. She couldn't stand it anymore. "So then what?"

"So I told Sean I didn't believe he sold his bike because he was worried about me, because he knows I can take care of myself." Nicki paused for dramatic effect. It worked. Jillian's eyebrows stood up and she was giving Nicki's story the attention it deserved. Hell, she was practically ready to wring it out of Nicki. "And then he kissed me."

"What?"

Nicki nodded. "Yeah, full on, tongue and all, and he wasn't wearing a shirt, and holy shit. It was like eight friggin' years just disappeared."

"Holy crap. Is he still with Kayla?"

"Yeah, and she walked in right after. Talk about timing. But before that, he was saying, 'That didn't happen,' like he hadn't just had his tongue in my mouth. And I said, 'Yeah, it did.' But Kayla showed up, so we couldn't talk about it. And that's pretty much where I left it." She took a deep breath. "So, expert of relationships, teller of the future, what do you think? Are you thinking what I'm thinking?"

She glanced at the clock on Jillian's wall. "And can you tell me in an hour or less, because Napoli awaits?"

CHAPTER THIRTEEN

NICKI SHOWERED WHEN she got home. She had to remove all the kid germs. It was worse than when she'd arrived at Jillian's, because she actually hugged and kissed all three kids before she came home, and she left with a sticky film covering herself from head to toe. There was some weird grape stain on her shirt that she was pretty sure would never come out. Ick. Maybe Nathan should have hosed her down when she left, kind of a decontamination chamber in the front yard, instead of upon her arrival.

But she got what she'd gone there for. She had her friend's perspective on the whole Sean thing, and it was what she'd needed. Nicki had actually started convincing herself that maybe she had a chance with Sean, but Jillian didn't think so. Jillian figured it was just because Nicki—one of Sean's closest friends—was getting all kinds of attention from this good-looking swarthy man right under Sean's nose, and it set off his primeval macho defenses. "It's thousands of years of evolution, Nicki. One alpha fights another for dominance over all the females. It's not that he cares about you that way, Nick. It's that he wants to be the rooster of us all. You're part of his brood and Carlos was sniffing around."

So, it completely sucked, but she could live with it.

And it got her to thinking that maybe too Sean was still struggling with his whole do-I-or-don't-I-move-in-with-Kayla dilemma, and maybe that kiss was his one last-ditch attempt at asserting his singleness.

Or he just wanted to fuck with her head.

Yeah, that was probably it.

So she spent the next twenty-four hours de-escalating the situation in her head, so that next time she saw him, she could be good old Nicki, friend extraordinaire.

Yeah, right. Sunday afternoon, about two o'clock, Nicki pulled her car in front of her parents' house. And in the end of the driveway sat Sean's blue Ford truck. She felt her body pump up with adrenaline to rise to the challenge, and that's when she realized she was still nowhere near ready to deal with Sean. But what was she gonna do? Not see her one and only brother? Didn't think so. She had to re-find that pair of balls she grew and strap 'em on. In front of the family, there was only one way to handle it: get along as best she could and pretend things were peachy. Ignore Sean as much as possible. Avoid eye contact when able. Deal with him the way he deserved later. Even if she was just one of his fictional hens and there was only friendship there, they needed to talk about it.

Why did mom even invite him? This was supposed to be a family thing.

But Sean was like family. Nicki knew that. Sean had

been a part of Will's life since Will's age was in the single digits. So Will had probably invited Sean himself. So be it. It was what it was, and she had to deal with it.

So she walked up the sidewalk to mom and dad's sunflower yellow house and rang the doorbell. As usual, though, she didn't wait for them to answer the door. Instead, she popped in and yelled, "Just me," then threw her purse on the bench in the entryway.

"Nini!" Will came from the living room and hugged his sister. When he'd learned to talk as a toddler, he'd said *Nicki* as *Nini*, and he'd never stopped calling her that. Nicki liked it because no one else had that name for her, just Will.

Every time Will came home, Nicki was surprised at how tall he was. He probably hadn't grown in five years, but the visits were few and far between, and Nicki still thought of Will as her little brother. Not so little, though. He was a good six inches taller than she was. "Baby brother!" His dark brown hair was trimmed but still longish, giving his hair a messy can't-be-bothered-with-my-hair look that she was sure some girls loved. He had cute dimples and dark brown eyes; his looks had hardly changed since he was seven. He would always be her baby brother. She wrapped her arms around him. "How the hell have you been, Mr. Smartypants?"

"Smartypants? What's that supposed to mean?"

"Would you prefer 'smartest guy in the world'?"

He smiled. "Ah. You'll need to meet my buddy Lex sometimes. Blows me away, man."

"Please. I can barely understand *you* half the time anymore." He locked her head in the crook of his elbow, then turned so they could start the journey into the other room. "Mmm. Smells good. Mom outdid herself as always."

"She put the roast on early. It was already halfway done when I got up this morning. She said that's her secret to tender beef that falls apart at the touch of the fork tines: Cook it to friggin' death."

"Nice." She breathed in the various smells wafting from the kitchen. "Nobody cooks like mom." They started walking, but Nicki wasn't sure where Will planned to go. To the left was the dining room, straight ahead was the kitchen, and to the right was the living room. Nicki, as a preemptive strike, bore full forward to head to the kitchen. Mom was sure to be there and Sean not. Sean was no doubt talking to dad in the living room. She was not ready.

Will didn't fight her lead. "Hey, mom," Nicki said, and hugged her mother. Carol Sosebee's blonde hair was tucked up into not quite a bun but some elaborate updo that might have been appropriate at a formal occasion. But it highlighted the length of her neck and the curvature of her jaw. When her mother wore her hair up, Nicki could tell she was her mother's daughter, even though she often joked that they must have adopted her. Even their light brown eyes looked nearly identical.

"Hi, honey." She stepped back toward the stove. "It's been a couple of weeks, and I'd swear you've lost weight."

Mom always said that. She smiled. "Not a pound, mom. I swear." She was wearing a hemp-green baby doll tee that said "Save the Planet" and short white shorts with white flip-flops. Maybe she needed to wear boy shirts stuffed with pillows and flared jeans. Then maybe mom would stop pestering her about her weight. Sheesh...if she'd really lost weight as often as mom thought she did, she'd weigh about twenty-three pounds by now. "So, what can I do to help?"

"Well, almost everything is ready. You and Will can take out all that stuff over there." She pointed to the small table in the kitchen. On the table sat a beautiful green salad full of cherry tomatoes and cucumbers, two small pitchers with salad dressings, a large carafe of ice water with thin slices of lemon floating in it, and a bowl full of warm rolls. Nicki grabbed the salad and one of the pitchers and walked to the dining room.

The table was already set. She could tell how much her mother missed Will when she saw the room. She was using her best china, real silverware, and linen tablecloths and napkins. In the center of the table was a vase full of various flowers professionally arranged. Nicki had no idea what any of them were (except for the baby's breath), but they were colorful and smelled sweet but not overpowering. Will followed with an armful that he placed on the table. "Mom really outdid herself, huh, isn't that what you said?"

"Yeah, overboard." She started walking back to the kitchen but turned around and smiled. "She really misses you."

He grinned, only a step behind her. "Yeah, she said she misses you too because you never visit."

Ouch. It was true, though. She tried to visit every two or three weeks, but it was hard. Besides being pretty busy, she was often lectured about her clothes, her habits, her jobs (and seeming slackeritis), her—*ahem*—expressive use of language, her choice of friends, her choice of man friends and frequency thereof, her refusal to go to church, and on and on and on. But she wasn't going to lay all that on Will. She chuckled. "I visit when you're here. You'll just have to come home more often."

He smiled as they returned to the kitchen. Mom had since put more food on the table to be carried to the dining room—a large bowl of green beans and another piled high with fluffy mashed potatoes. Nicki felt her stomach grumble. She hadn't eaten yet. As she picked up the bowl of mashed potatoes, she realized she hadn't even heard her dad and Sean.

When Will and Nicki returned to the kitchen yet again, mom said, "Will, honey, I need to get this roast on the platter. Can you tilt the pan and I'll get it out?" He obliged and came over to the stove to help her. "Nicki, would you get your father and Sean and ask them to wash up?"

Shit. Just her luck. "Yeah, if I knew where they were."

Will grinned. "They're in the backyard. Dad got a riding lawnmower and is showing it off. He's just like Tim Allen in *Home Improvement*."

Nicki laughed and did her best imitation of Tim Allen's character. In a deep voice she said, "Ah...needs more power!" Will shook his head, smiling, and Nicki walked to the door at the end of the kitchen. As she got closer, she saw through the door that—on the right side of the yard—dad certainly was showing Sean his shiny new red lawnmower. *Suck it up, Nicki.* She walked out the door and was blasted by the warm air. She hadn't realized how cool it was inside until she came back out.

She gritted her jaw. Sean's back was to her, but he looked good as always. He was wearing a black t-shirt and a newer pair of blue jeans. His hair, not contained by his usual work do-rag, was slicked back. God, his hair always looked so hot like that. No way could she stand being around him today. Well, she *could* just shout from the door, right? Or maybe she could behave and act like an adult. She did need to give her dad a hug after all. Then maybe she could feign a stomach bug and go home. She used to be an actress in high school, so surely she could pull that off.

She took a deep breath and walked toward them. Dad looked up from the lawnmower where he'd been showing Sean some feature that probably adjusted the blades an eighth of an inch at a time. "There's my Nicki girl." He held open his arms. Nicki might have looked like her mom, but Will was the spitting image of his dad—dark hair and eyes and way tall, so when Nicki hugged him, her head nestled his chest. Dad's hair was getting a little salt in it, but the dark hair still overpowered the light.

"Hi, dad." True test next. She glanced over—quickly, but not too fast, and then back to dad. "Sean." Cool but not cold. Whew. She did it. Dad pulled her in a close embrace. She could smell his usual Old Spice. She loved that smell. "Mom sent me out to tell you guys to wash up for lunch."

"Good. I'm hungry." He paused. "I just need to go move the water on the roses. Tell your mom I'll be right in."

Thanks, dad. That meant that she and Sean were alone to walk in together. Dad started heading around to the side of the house. She started walking toward the back door—not too fast, because she didn't want the need to escape to be so obvious. Sean, right behind her said, "What? No hug for me?"

For some reason, that hit her all kinds of wrong. She stopped in her tracks and took a deep breath. She had no idea what words were going to spew out of her mouth, but something was coming and there was no stopping it. She turned to her side where Sean now stood. She managed to make eye contact but she kept her voice low so no one else could hear, even though she talked quickly. "I have a better idea. Why don't you French me again?" She raised her eyebrows in mock surprise. "Oh, wait. I forgot that never happened. Never mind. Sorry." And before he could retort, she opened the back door and walked inside.

CHAPTER FOURTEEN

TALK ABOUT AWKWARD. Sean had taken the hint and wasn't forcing Nicki to engage in conversation. She knew what she'd done outside was immature, but what was he thinking? That she really *could* forget it? The problem was that Nicki just didn't know how to handle her feelings. If he was an ex-boyfriend, it would be no problem to burn a bridge, but Sean was a friend that she wanted to keep (and maybe the future love of her life); she just wasn't ready to deal civilly with him right now. The last time they'd been face to face he'd literally been *in* her face, and it was hard to pretend that hadn't happened. But snapping at him had worked. His expression outside had changed from amused to abashed (if she was reading him right) in short order, and she'd walked inside so fast, she didn't know what else he could have been thinking.

Worse yet, mom and dad were at both ends of the table as usual, but Will had insisted that Nicki *not* sit next to him as she'd wished, because he wanted to face her. That's why he wanted Sean on the other side of the table as well. So Nicki and Sean were sitting right next to each other. Close enough that the ceiling fan kept blowing the scent of his aftershave her way. If she hadn't been so pissed at him (and she hadn't realized until a few minutes ago just how angry she was), she would have loved it.

She wondered why Sean hadn't brought Kayla along with him, and then realized that his invitation to dinner was no doubt as last minute as hers had been. Kayla might have had other plans. Just as well, she thought. Kayla was a nice girl, but there was no substance to her. If Will had wanted to talk substance, Kayla probably couldn't have kept up.

"Mrs. Sosebee, would you please pass the mashed potatoes?" Sean asked her mom. Normally, Nicki would have smiled at Sean's formality with her parents; he still called them *Mr.* and *Mrs.* like he had in high school (of course, Nicki did the same with his mom), an unshakeable lovable habit.

"Certainly, Sean." She smiled and handed him the bowl.

"Everything smells really good. I don't get cooking like this very often." Nicki felt herself simmering beside him. Oh, really? Even from your "come home to a hot cooked meal" girl? Maybe Kayla's hot cooked meals came out of the microwave. Or maybe her hot cooked meals weren't actually meals at all. Nicki poured a little of mom's homemade raspberry vinaigrette on her salad and bit her bottom lip so hard she thought it might bleed, so she willed herself to relax.

A faint sigh escaped mom's lips as Sean spooned out the potatoes and she spied his knuckles. "Oh, Sean, I wish you'd get that dreadful BAMF tattoo removed." She said

BAMF just like in the old comic books, causing Nicki to smile.

Sean's lady killer smile curved his lips as he looked at Nicki's mom. "I've had it for seven years now. You're not used to it yet?"

"I'm *used* to it. It doesn't mean I like it." She handed Sean the bowl of green beans. "What does your mother think about it?"

Nicki allowed herself to look over at Sean. He was sitting in the figurative seat she usually occupied at her parents' house. But he seemed cool under the pressure. "She knows it's part of an image I have to maintain."

Not wanting to disrupt the flow, Nicki picked up the bowl of mashed potatoes from between the two of them but kept her gaze on Sean. She'd never heard this before.

"Image? Why do you need an image?"

Sean smiled again. "I own a motorcycle repair shop, Mrs. Sosebee. If I looked like Mister Rogers, no one would take me seriously, and my business would go under." Mom seemed to consider what he said. "If I look and dress the part, I'm halfway to being thought of as legitimate by the people who hire me to do the work. And then my work can speak for itself."

Dad chimed in. "How *is* business these days, Sean?"

Sean looked over to dad and so Nicki took her eyes off him. Didn't want him to have to satisfaction of knowing she was even paying attention. She handed the mashed potatoes to dad. "Keeps me busy." She folded her hands in front of her plate, waiting to see when Sean would set down the bowl of beans he was holding, but all her peripheral vision saw was him holding them suspended above the area. Shit. He wanted her to take them from him. So she looked up, barely caught his eye, then took the beans and began slowly spooning them onto her plate. "I actually had a really good week." Nicki saw her dad nod. "I sold my custom Harley a few days ago and made off it what I usually earn in six months, so I've now had my best year ever."

Holy shit. Nicki wondered how much the damned thing cost. And that meant that Carlos must have had a lot of money too. Maybe Sean was right about the gang thing, but she didn't want to know.

Sean continued talking. "So now I'm considering doing that on the side. I loved that bike, but the money I made on it was crazy, more than I would have thought I could."

It was a sore spot, but Nicki had to know. It meant she actually had to talk to him which was probably okay since he was handing her the butter. "Was it worth it, though? I mean, look at all the labor you put into it."

God, she could barely stand the way his eyes were drilling into hers. Could the rest of the family *see that*? "It was a labor of love, Nicki. But, really, that's when I considered her mine. If I was just building custom bikes knowing I was going to sell them, I wouldn't put that much time into them."

At least he'd admitted it. He hadn't wanted to part with that bike. He'd loved *her*, probably had even had a name for her that he hadn't told anyone else. Nicki knew how much that bike had meant to him, and so she couldn't quite let it go. "But you loved that bike, Sean. How could you just part with it like that?"

She'd hit a nerve. He picked up his glass of water and

took a sip. Then he looked her way but didn't look *at* her. "Sometimes you sacrifice for things that are more important."

And what the fuck was that supposed to mean? She couldn't very well grill him here. She could just picture that...Sean bringing up the fact that Nicki had been sleeping with Carlos, an alleged gang member. That wouldn't fly with her family. So she nodded her head, letting it go for now, and buttered her roll. No one else questioned it either. Then again, thanks to Nicki, the tension was thick in the air.

And it was quiet. Will saved the day. "Hey, Nini. Mom showed me your front page article. Great job, sis."

She looked up and smiled, silently thanking her brother. "First one."

Sean exhaled so that Nicki heard it. "Shit, Nicki, I didn't know. Sorry. Congratulations."

Nicki smiled at him, feeling sad that things were so strained between them right now. She wanted to say *sorry* back. "Thanks, Sean."

He looked over at her mother. "Can I read your copy later?"

"Of course."

Sean turned back to Nicki. "Is this the story you were telling me about the other day?"

She nodded. "Yeah. I don't think I told you the latest developments, and there's sure to be more next week."

Her dad said, "We're all proud of you, kiddo. Nice job."

She turned to face him and smiled. "Thanks, dad."

Will grinned. "Hey, I'm a writer too, you know."

Nicki tilted her head, smiling. "What do you write, baby

bro?"

Will feigned a disgusted look. "Perhaps you've heard of a *master's thesis?*"

"Well, yeah, but what is that exactly?"

"It's huge, and if you can't write one, you don't get your master's degree. I don't expect you to read it all, but I'll bring my copy home next time I'm here. It's one-hundred-and-thirty-three pages of heterodox economics genius."

"Of *what?*" Nicki's smile grew. Will was moving into the area where she wouldn't be able to keep up with him.

"Let's just say, sis, that I impressed the hell out of my thesis committee and graduated with honors."

The remainder of the day was much more relaxed, and Sean and Nicki had reached a silent understanding. They didn't talk much, but it was apparent that no one else knew there was something weird going on. All of them moved from dinner to dessert and then everyone pitched in to clean the dishes and put the leftover food away. Sean read the newspaper article and saw its placement on the front page, on the right hand side, just below the fold. He muttered something about having to buy the paper now. Then they all played Monopoly and Will used the game as an excuse to talk about everything he'd learned in the last several years. Nicki loved to see his passion for it, and she knew he was going into the right field. Will admitted that his ultimate goal was to teach economics, because he found it so fascinating.

The one game lasted into the early evening and mom insisted on feeding everyone again. This time, though, they just had roast beef sandwiches and chips, because no one was famished. They started playing Trivial Pursuit and didn't finish it either, because as the night wore on and it got really late, and Nicki said she had to head home. She planned on moving into full investigative reporter mode on Monday, and Mondays were also the day she worked her makeup business, so she wanted to get a good night's sleep.

Sean said that he should probably go too and timed it so that they walked out together. And instead of walking toward his truck, Sean walked Nicki to her car in front of the house. She didn't say anything, just fished her hand around in her purse, feeling for her keys. Sean asked, "You still mad at me?"

They stopped on the sidewalk, able to see each other's faces because of the ambient glow of the street light and the porch light from her parents' house. They were under the shade of a tree, so it wasn't like they were under a spotlight but they had enough light to see. Nicki felt a cool breeze, and she wondered if it was going to rain tonight. It didn't matter, really, because one thing she had always loved about her area of Colorado was that evenings in Winchester almost always cooled down enough to be comfortable, no matter how hot the day had been.

Her keys in hand, she looked at Sean. It was time to talk, no matter if she was ready or not. The time was right. She shook her head. "No, I'm not mad." Not anymore, anyway. She looked down at the keys, though, because it was hard to look at him.

"Hey, I'm sorry, okay? I don't know what happened the other day, and it will never happen again."

Fuck, Sean, don't promise that. That's why it had torn her up so much, because she'd dreamed of that for how long? And he hadn't disappointed in his technique. But it was clear from his words that he did want everything to go back to "normal." And Nicki knew, just like the time they shook hands and agreed to pretend they had never slept together—The Night—that she was at a crossroads…either make nice and play the game or say goodbye forever.

She couldn't say goodbye.

So instead she had to accept that Sean would always and only just be her friend. She shook her head and looked up. "It's cool." And that was it.

CHAPTER FIFTEEN

SHE'D WANTED TO ask so much more, to really talk about it, but Sean's voice indicated that he wasn't willing to go there. She would never know exactly why Sean had kissed her at that moment or why he had *sacrificed* (to use his words) his bike on her account. She wouldn't know if he really had deeper feelings for her. As she lay in bed awake that night into the early morning, she finally decided that Sean must know on some level that she still had those feelings for him, and he'd kissed her to make her forget about Carlos. If she was right, then Sean was even smarter than she'd given him credit for. That would mean he knew Nicki almost better than she knew herself, that he knew her motivations, her desires, her urges.

But that's what friends did, right? They *knew* their friends well.

And yet tonight Nicki had learned something about Sean that she'd never thought about, so what did that say about *her* as a friend? Had her eyes been so clouded by her strong emotions that she sometimes just thought about Sean in a sexual way, not considering him in full dimension? She had known Sean was careful about his "image," to use his own word. He'd always been attentive to his looks, but Nicki had always imagined it was just because he wanted to look good, seemingly for the girls. But she'd seen tonight that Sean had some business savvy, and that—while girls did cream themselves over how he looked—what he had done was calculated on a whole other level. She found that this knowledge gave her new respect for her friend.

And that didn't help one bit with the way she felt.

So tomorrow, she told herself, as her thoughts finally started to wind down, she was going to focus on work and on finding another boyfriend who could rock her world so hard that Sean really could feel like just a friend.

Thanks to her mind's refusal to let her sleep as she should have, she slept later than she'd wanted. As she ate a piece of buttered toast for breakfast, she sketched out a to do list that included calling one-fourth of her makeup customers to see if they needed anything, then calling Charles Baker—Jason Edwards's arson victim—and Melissa Jacobs, currently starring in the role of Helen of Troy.

She showered and dressed, did her hair and makeup, then sat at the kitchen table with her little book of customer names and numbers. She didn't work her makeup business too hard anymore, but she had close to forty loyal customers, and Nicki herself got her makeup at fifty percent off because of it, so it was hard to give it up. She called nine numbers and left five voice mail messages. The other four she was able to speak with, and only one needed anything right now. She asked for black waterproof mascara and charcoal eyeliner. Nicki kept a small inventory on the top shelf of her closet, and those were two products she knew she had plenty of. She promised to drop them off later in the day.

Then she knew she had to get on to reporting duties. She fired up her laptop computer anticipating she might need it for research. She still had the arrest affidavit on the table and skimmed through it. It had an address for Baker (the one with the burned house) but no phone number. But when she did an online search for Charles Baker at that address, she got a phone number in the time it took to press enter. Without hesitation, she picked up her cell phone and dialed.

She got his voice mail. She wasn't too surprised, because she figured his landline hadn't survived the fire anymore than his house had. She left a message, telling him that she was a reporter for the *Winchester Tribune* investigating the Jason Edwards case and would like to ask him a few questions.

Well, she hadn't made much progress so far, and she didn't want to lose the momentum she'd had last week. So she searched for Melissa Jacobs's phone number and also found it online. Apparently the woman had a landline at her home in Winchester. Now Nicki was getting somewhere.

Her phone rang before she could dial, though. The number belonged to one of her makeup customers that she'd left a message with just minutes ago. "Hi, Sheri. How are you?"

"Nicki, I think I do want to order some stuff, but I want a new look for summer. I don't suppose you could come over later and give me a facial?"

She was torn, but she was pretty free, all things considered. "What about tonight? Do you have anything going on?"

Sheri thought for a moment. "No, I think I could do it. What time are you thinking?"

"I don't know. Sometime after five." Her inner saleswoman kicked in. "And—as you know—if you invite some friends, I can discount whatever you buy."

She could hear the smile in Sheri's voice. "How about seven, and I see how many girlfriends I can get to come over?"

"Sounds good. I'll be there around six to set up." More potential customers were always good, considering Nicki had never quite been able to give up selling makeup.

She then called Melissa Jacobs's number. It rang several times but was finally answered by a woman. After confirming the woman was Jacobs, Nicki introduced herself as a reporter from the *Tribune* who wanted to ask her some questions about the Edwards case.

"Um, I really don't have anything to say, and I don't want to talk about it."

In her short time as a reporter, Nicki had rarely been given the "no comment" line, but it seemed to be happening more and more. This woman hadn't quite said it yet, though, and Nicki sensed she had a chance. "I just want to ask you a couple of questions so readers know your perspective."

She heard the woman sigh. "Let me think about it."

That was good enough for Nicki. Nicki was going to give the woman her phone number and ask her to call back, but then she knew it would be too easy to be blown off that way. Instead, Nicki promised to call Jacobs back tomorrow for her final answer.

Well, so much for doing a lot of reporter-type work today. At least tomorrow she could sit in court again. Tuesdays had turned out to be the best days to sit in, and at least once a month she would find something worth writing about. Maybe it was for the best since she'd committed to an evening of makeup. She got out her presentation bag and made sure her tools and supplies were in order.

Before Nicki left her apartment to deliver makeup to one customer and do a facial party for the other, she got a call from Charles Baker.

"Mr. Baker, I'd like to interview you regarding the Jason Edwards case."

"Look, ma'am, I realize you're just doing your job, but I've really had enough of the drama your town has brought me. Oh, uh, that's off the record. If you want to quote anything from me, it can be 'no comment.' No offense, but I've had enough."

Nicki was not surprised. "None taken. Thank you for your time."

Man, if she couldn't get Melissa Jacobs to agree to an interview, she was back at square one. She'd have to wait for Edwards's trial or until the authorities found Michael Sterne. She had no choice but to sit in court tomorrow morning and hope for another promising story.

By the end of the evening, she'd had all the girl time she could stand. She liked helping women make themselves look pretty, but so many questions and hesitations about what to buy and how much to spend wore her out. All told, though, she earned about seventy dollars net on Sheri's five friends, and Sheri scored a thirty-percent discount herself. And, if these women were anything like the women from previous facial parties, at least two of them would also become loyal customers in the future. So it was worth the time.

The next morning, Nicki sat in court and struck out. She was getting discouraged. That afternoon, though, she called Melissa Jacobs again. When the woman answered the phone, Nicki reintroduced herself. "Is there any way you would consider an interview?"

The woman hesitated but said, "Okay. You can come over to my house tomorrow. How about eleven?"

Nicki would have cheered out loud if it wouldn't have made her seem unprofessional and then cause her to lose the interview. "That sounds great, Ms. Jacobs." The woman gave Nicki her address and Nicki recorded it in her steno book. Yes!

She started to dial Sean's number and then hesitated. Damn it. It was just like the aftermath of The Night. There was an awkwardness between them again, and she felt like she couldn't call him or go by and see him when something cool happened like she used to. Part of her wanted to just decide that was it, that there was nothing to save there, but she really couldn't bear the thought of Sean not being in her life at all.

Maybe tomorrow she'd just go over to his garage and try to break the ice. Somehow.

CHAPTER SIXTEEN

SEAN TOOK THE pressure off Nicki himself. That evening, Sean and two of his close male friends showed up at Napoli and requested Nicki as their waitress. When Mandy told her she had a table of three (and had neglected to tell her they'd specifically requested Nicki as their waitress), she was surprised to see them.

This particular Tuesday night was slower than usual, so Nicki didn't have to make the table wait. She came out of the server area and didn't quite know what to think when she saw Jesse, Sean's friend since middle school, and Travis, one of his biker friends, one he'd hit it off with shortly after opening his business.

She spotted Jesse at her table first as he was facing her and then she saw Travis, because she could see him in profile, but Sean's back was to her. It didn't take her much time to figure out who he was when she saw Jesse and Travis, but she would have recognized Sean anywhere. Except instead of wearing his hair slicked back like he did a lot of times, he was wearing it loose. She hadn't seen him wear it that way in a long time, so she was curious to see how he looked up close.

More than that, though, she thought as each footstep brought her closer to their table, what did it mean that he and his friends came to Nicki's turf? It was already apparent to her that they'd asked for Nicki to be their waitress, so what did it mean? Why were they there? Well, *stupid*, it didn't mean a goddamn thing. It wasn't the first time Sean had been to Napoli, nor was it the first time he'd requested Nicki as a waitress. In fact, just a few months ago, it had been with Kayla. *Get over it.*

And *be cool*. She got to their table, her waitress smile on her face. "What a pleasant surprise. Good to see you guys. Are you thirsty?"

Travis grinned. He had hair that was black as a raven and emerald green eyes. The guy was an ass, as far as Nicki was concerned, but he was easy on the eyes. He was the most heavily tattooed of the three at the table, and he wore a sleeveless shirt to show them off. "Have you been outside lately? I'd say me and the boys are dehydrated."

"Then pick your poison."

Sean spoke up. "We'll get a pitcher. Coors all right, guys?"

"Yep." Travis looked up from the menu again. "Just keep it comin'."

Nicki smiled. "I think I can do that. Any appetizers?"

Jesse finally joined the conversation. "Why don't we get some of that garlic bread with mozzarella? That's pretty killer." Jesse and Nicki had always gotten along, even during that awkward period in high school when he kept hitting on her in spite of the fact that she had a steady boyfriend. But Sean took care of that. Jesse wasn't a bad-looking guy—brown hair, brown eyes, with a similar build and stature to Sean. He wasn't as concerned about his looks as Sean, though—he seemed more laid back about it. He had a couple of tats on his arms, a couple of ear piercings, and an eyebrow piercing that Nicki had told him was a great move right after he'd had it done.

Sean and Travis nodded. "Okay. I'll get the kitchen on that, and I'll be right back with your beer."

As she stepped away from the table, she breathed a sigh of relief. She'd done it and not freaked out. But her hands started shaking, some weird after-adrenaline rush surging through her veins. And she knew why. Jesus, it was like Sean was a fucking male model. His hair was perfectly tousled, touching his eyebrows without hanging in and covering up his eyes. *Très* sexy. How did he do that? How did he manage to up the hot factor every time she saw him?

She punched in the order for the cheese bread, then went to the bar.

Only tonight she was stuck with the lame bartender. Nicki didn't mind getting her own drinks, but it pissed her off when it wasn't necessary. Tonight Amy was the bartender and she was sitting on the customer side of the bar flirting with the one guy there, watching the big screen TV on the wall with him. Nicki pulled a pitcher out of the freezer, noting that the poor guy didn't seem to be enjoying her company. Unfortunately for him, Nicki didn't want to waste time helping to extricate him from Amy's verbal clutches.

Amy noticed Nicki. "Hey, I can get that." And…how

long would Nicki have to wait? No thanks.

"No worries. I got it." If Nicki were slammed with tables, she would have insisted.

"Suit yourself." Amy turned her attention back to the customer. That was *not* what they meant by customer service, but she wasn't Amy's boss. And she didn't want to be. She saw the shit the supervisors had to put up with here, and she wanted no part of it. But the crappy supervisors allowed people like Amy to get away with murder. And in spite of supervisors, Nicki had learned over the years that there were a variety of people she would always be stuck working with: *slackers* who only did the least amount of work they could get away with (Amy was half slacker); *reverse golden rulers* who asked what was in it for them (this was Amy's other half), as though their paycheck wasn't enough; *Nazis* who wanted things done one way and one way only, even if there were multiple ways to do a particular job; and *whiners* who would do their job but complain about how hard it was. No matter where she'd worked, she always had to deal with these personalities. The customers were easy; the coworkers were not. And the less she had to deal with the slackers, reverse golden rulers, Nazis, and whiners, the better. So she poured the beer herself.

When she got back to their table, Sean, Travis, and Jesse's menus were closed, indicating to Nicki that they were ready to put in their pizza order. As she slid the tray on the table to pour them their first beers, she asked, "Did you guys already hear the specials or do you even care?"

She handed the first glass of beer she poured to Travis, since he was seated the farthest away, then Jesse to her left and Sean to her right.

"No, we're ready to order." Sean looked up at Nicki, his eyes and smile relaxed. He seemed *different*. His hair, maybe?

"Shoot."

"We're gonna have a large double pepperoni."

"Thick or thin?"

Sean raised his eyebrows and looked over at the other two. Jesse said, "Thick."

Sean nodded and handed the menu to Nicki. She took the other menus as well. "I'll get that out as soon as it's ready."

And then business picked up. She didn't have time to talk much, but she brought out their appetizer and then their pizza, followed shortly by another pitcher of beer. As the evening wound down, they asked for yet another pitcher and had her box up the last two slices of pizza. But they stayed, nursing one pitcher of beer after another. They started getting a little louder but not rowdy. Finally, they were the only table left in Nicki's section, and she and the other two waitresses had finished almost all their closing duties except for the floor, which had to wait until all customers were gone.

Since everything was done, Nicki decided she could spend some time with Sean and his friends. "How's everything, guys?"

They were all feeling good, had just finished a good laugh, and all had wide smiles on their faces. "Great."

Sean asked, "Are we keeping you from getting your stuff done?"

"Nope. You can stay here till ten, and then I'll kick your

asses out."

All three laughed. Oh, yeah, they were feeling pretty damned good. Jesse asked, "What time is it?"

"It's about nine-thirty. You still have time."

"Should we get one more?"

Sean waved his hand close to the table. "No. I'm good."

"Me too." Travis picked up the pitcher. "Besides, there's still a little left."

Jesse held out his glass. "Then it's mine." While Travis poured the remaining beer in his glass, Jesse looked back up at Nicki. "Why don't you join us for a little bit?"

It was tempting. She didn't usually sit down with customers, but it was dead and there was nothing left to do. And God knew where the other waitresses were. Probably smoking behind the restaurant. And if any customers came in, she could stand and take care of them before they even realized she'd been sitting down. "Okay." She pulled out the chair and sat. "So what are you guys up to tonight?"

Sean wasted no time answering. "Just hanging out."

"Ah, a little guy time and here I am messing all that up."

Jesse slammed his glass down. He might have been a little drunk, but he managed to play sober well…except for slamming the glass. "We invited you. I'd ask if you wanted a drink, but…"

Nicki smiled. "I can't drink on the job anyway."

Sean said, "I told the guys about your front-page article."

Nicki felt her cheeks grow warm. "I'm pretty proud of that." Jesse shifted in his chair and his knee started digging into the outside of her thigh by her knee. She scootched the chair over a little to break the contact.

Travis said, "Yeah, I saw that article and read it, but I guess I didn't catch that you were the one who wrote it. This was your first one?"

"Yep. Well, first time on the front page." There was Jesse's knee again. What the fuck? She got ready to move her chair over again and give him a dirty look but turned her face to him first. He had a shit-eating grin on his face; he was *fucking* with her—actually, *flirting* might be a better way to describe it. But to what end? So instead of moving her chair, Nicki playfully pushed his knee off her leg by pushing her leg against his with force. They smiled at each other and he winked at her.

I'll be damned. Sean's friend had a crush on Nicki again. Maybe he was as pathetic as Nicki was—maybe he'd never gotten over her any better than she'd gotten over Sean.

And then she had an epiphany. She knew all about the *bros before hos* motto and wondered how Sean would feel about that. She didn't know how much Jesse knew about what had happened between Sean and Nicki. Sean and Jesse were really good friends, so surely he had heard about The Night and Nicki's embarrassing faux pas. He probably had *not* heard the latest, but Nicki couldn't even pretend to imagine what guys talked about when they were alone. Maybe he had.

And maybe Jesse knew that Nicki was only a friend to Sean.

But maybe Nicki would have to test that out. Just how would Sean feel if she dated (or even just slept with) one of his close male friends? She'd never done it before.

She might have to find out. Soon.

But for now, back to chatting them all up and then she had to get back to work. "Anyway, tomorrow I have an interview with Melissa Jacobs."

Jesse asked, "Who's that?"

Nicki gave Jesse the background on Jacobs and told the guys that she thought Jacobs might be able to give her a lot of good information. Another front page article perhaps? That was the plan.

Sean hugged Nicki when the guys left at ten. They were going next door to the sports bar because they weren't ready for the night to be over. Jesse forced a hug on Nicki as well. Between that and the huge tip on the table, Jesse was now in her crosshairs.

CHAPTER SEVENTEEN

NICKI DIDN'T KNOW what to wear to her interview with Melissa Jacobs. Sometimes she wore cute dresses to court, and sometimes she wore business-type suits to some interviews, but she wasn't sure what would feel most appropriate in this particular situation.

She spent far too long standing at the closet, but she finally settled on a light white cotton dress, one with short sleeves, a skirt that came to her knees, and a pair of white sandals. Conservative for Nicki, but appropriate for interviewing a woman who was no doubt nervous and upset. Nicki had written down a few questions but planned to wing a good part of it. She preferred following her gut instincts. She mainly wanted to know all the events that had led up to Edwards's arrest.

She arrived at Melissa Jacobs's modest home just a couple of minutes early. The woman lived in a small house in one of the lower-income neighborhoods of Winchester. There were no trees around the house and no lawn. There were small weeds in the front yard that had no doubt been mowed down recently. There was no fence around the house and just a makeshift driveway on the left side. There were two vehicles parked there—one an old light blue Chevy pickup that had seen better days and a burgundy Subaru station wagon (also old). Nicki's Jetta would feel at home here.

She parked in front of the house. She left her purse on the floor of her car, taking with her her keys, pad and pen, and cell phone (which she tucked into her right hand pocket). She locked the door and turned around, taking in her surroundings. Jacobs's home itself wasn't that spectacular either. It was white but part of the paint was peeling in spots. She walked up the stone path (someone at some time had cared for this home, but she didn't think it was the current occupant). There was evidence that at one time there had been a screen door on the place but not anymore. The doorbell was also missing its cover. Nicki felt bad that this poor woman couldn't afford upkeep for the place or, if she was renting, that the landlord didn't give enough of a shit to fix things.

She knocked on the door—it had a window that was covered with a white and light yellow gingham curtain. She noted that the window way over to the right also had heavy drapes that were closed. Apparently Jacobs valued her privacy.

A slight breeze drifted past her legs. Nicki was glad it was overcast today. By the looks of this house, she didn't expect air conditioning inside. She glanced around the neighborhood. There wasn't much activity right now—no dogs barking, no kids playing, no cars driving by. It was quiet.

Nicki was starting to suspect that Jacobs had changed her mind. But if she was here, Nicki wasn't going to leave without trying more than once. She knocked on the door again, and she'd call the woman's phone if need be.

At last, Nicki heard the doorknob turning. Maybe the woman hadn't heard the first time Nicki knocked. Nicki inhaled deeply and put on her reporter face.

The woman who opened the door had her light brown hair pulled back into a ponytail. She wasn't wearing any makeup and looked tired. Or stressed. Nicki wasn't quite sure which. She wanted Melissa Jacobs to feel at ease with her, so she wouldn't become more stressed with the questions she'd get around to asking. So she put on a friendly but not overbearing smile. "Ms. Melissa Jacobs?" The woman nodded her head. "Hi. I'm Nicki Sosebee with the *Winchester Tribune*. We spoke on the phone yesterday."

"Yes."

Nicki stood there, waiting for the woman to invite her in, but she simply stood in the doorway. "Um, as I said on the phone, I'd like to ask you some questions. Can I come in for a few moments?"

The woman seemed a little nervous. "Can't you just ask me here?"

Nicki had to put her at ease. She smiled. "You might get tired of just standing here, don't you think? And I want to make sure I quote you properly, so it would be best if I could take notes somewhere." She decided to try a different tactic. "Can I maybe take you out for a cup of coffee?" To clarify, she added, "My treat."

"Well, I need to be here for my sons."

Kids? Oh, okay. But she needed this interview. How could she entice this woman to talk, really talk? "McDonalds, then?"

Jacobs was uncomfortable. "How long do you think this will take?"

Nicki scrunched up her mouth, then said, "Ten minutes at the most, I think."

The woman sighed. "Then why don't you just come in and let's get this over with?"

Well, that's what Nicki liked. A good attitude. This was going to be a great interview. *Not.*

Nicki followed Jacobs into a small kitchen. The room, just like the outside, had seen better days. The floor was covered in linoleum that had a brown and yellow pattern, no doubt popular eons ago, and it was pock-marked with cooking mishaps and furniture wounds. The walls were off white, but the window facing the driveway had the same yellow-and-white gingham curtains. These were open and letting in a little light, but the overhead light was turned on. In the center of the small room was a white-and-gold-flecked Formica-topped table, no doubt kept from the era the linoleum came from. Nicki felt like she'd stepped into the past.

Nicki noticed a few dishes piled in the sink but nothing outrageous. The home—though worn down—appeared to be pretty clean. She stood beside the table, not feeling welcome enough to just sit down. Finally, though, Jacobs pulled a chair out and indicated with a wave of her hand that Nicki should sit down as well. So…no formalities, no foreplay. Just get to it and get out.

"Okay, Ms. Jacobs," she said as she opened her steno pad. "I have just a few questions. Because I want to be fair and impartial, I might ask some questions that seem to have obvious answers, but I don't want to just jump to conclusions. I'd rather hear the answers from you." Nicki said this, because she had already formulated her own opinion. She suspected that Michael Sterne, Melissa Jacobs's ex-boyfriend and half-brother of Jason Edwards, was jealous of Jacobs's relationship with Charles Baker. What that relationship was, only Jacobs could tell her. But she wanted to hear what Jacobs herself had to say. "According to Jason Edwards's arrest affidavit, he and your ex-boyfriend Michael Sterne are suspected of setting fire to Charles Baker's home in Colorado Springs. What is your involvement in all this?"

"What do you mean, 'involvement'?"

"I don't mean that you were directly involved. I mean more like where did you fit into all of it?"

"Well, I don't know if you know, but Mike and I were together for a long time...eight or nine years. He's the boys' dad. Anyway, we separated, and then I was dating Charles for a time. Charles came here to visit me and he and Mike got into a fight. Right out there in front of the house. And if the neighbors hadn't called the cops, they probably would have worked it out without anybody getting in trouble."

Okay, that was weird. Nicki hadn't studied domestic violence much, but this woman definitely sounded like a victim. She'd obviously had the balls to leave the jerk in the first place (and, if he was anything like his little brother, Nicki could only imagine what a piece of work he was) but could never really get away.

"So are you still dating Mr. Baker?"

Jacobs's eyes widened. "No." She didn't intend to expand on her answer.

"So why do you think Edwards actually set fire to Baker's house? Do you think it was to keep the police from suspecting your ex of being involved, Ms. Jacobs?"

The woman raised her eyebrows. "You can call me Melissa." She lowered her voice and leaned over the table. "Have you ever met Jason? Does he seem stable to you?"

Nicki rolled her eyes. "Yes, I've met him and, frankly, he scared the hell out of me."

"So you don't think he might have been tempted to do that all on his own?"

"But why would he, Melissa? Did he have an axe to grind with you or with Baker?"

Melissa looked down at her hands and then shrugged. "No, not really. Not that I know of."

"Does he have a prior relationship with you that would make him act like a jealous ex?"

Melissa swallowed hard. "Heavens, no."

Nicki was missing something here, that much she knew. Melissa Jacobs was forthcoming, but something just wasn't right. Nicki knew it in her bones. But how to get to the core of the truth? That she didn't know.

And then it hit her. What if this woman were still under her ex's thumb, fugitive or no, and...? *Holy shit.* What if she knew where he was?

And how did Nicki ask that question?

She would ask it the only way she knew how—straight and to the point: "Ms. Jacobs...I mean, Melissa, do you have any idea where Michael Sterne might be?"

Nicki imagined Sterne and Edwards camping out at their mother's place, bullying her into whatever it was they wanted. She couldn't forget the short few seconds she'd spent with their mother and the disrespectful, antagonistic way Edwards had treated the woman who'd given birth to him. And if Sterne were that close by, surely Melissa Jacobs would know it.

But if she did, she wasn't going to admit it. "Why would you think I'd have any idea?" Nicki's pen was poised on her steno pad, but she hadn't looked down at it in a while. She was glad she hadn't, because she wouldn't have noticed the way Melissa's eyes darted toward the living room. The woman hadn't done it intentionally, but Nicki was no idiot and had grown proficient at reading body language.

And if Nicki understood her correctly, Michael Sterne was in Melissa Jacobs's house, right here, right now.

CHAPTER EIGHTEEN

NICKI WAS AN expert at playing it cool. She had to do it almost every night at work, and hell, she did it with Sean on a weekly basis. She knew she had to keep a level head right now, especially if her theory was correct.

So, if Sterne was hiding out in this house, with or without Melissa's permission, Nicki was like a doe walking into the midst of a dozen blaze orange jackets on the first day of deer season. It all made sense now, why Melissa had been willing to do the interview yesterday and then reluctant today, not even willing to let Nicki into her house.

Nicki took a deep breath to give herself time to think. How did she leave gracefully, and—more importantly—quickly, without arousing suspicion? She looked down at her steno pad, pretending to jot a note, then moved her eyes over the page and flipping back one, just to give the impression that she was trying to be thorough. As to rescuing this woman, if Sterne really was in her home, she'd ask her editor how he would handle that. Or maybe she could call the stupid detective she'd visited last week. In the meantime, there would be no rescue if she couldn't remove herself from the situation. "Well, Melissa, I think you've answered all the questions I have today. Can I give you a call if I have other questions later on?"

Melissa's eyes seemed to relax. Oh, yeah, Nicki was right. Melissa was safer if she could get Nicki out, so she was as relieved as Nicki, even though the woman tried to hide it. She pushed her chair out from behind her. "Oh, sure, that would be fine."

A tall, skinny man with dark hair intertwined with silver strands and darker eyes entered from the living room, a gun in hand. Nicki recognized Sterne from his description. *Shit.* Not fast enough. And did he look pissed. "I don't think so." He pointed the gun directly at Nicki. What did he plan to do? "You're staying right here until I figure out what to do with you, reporter girl." He walked over to the door, drawing the gingham curtain aside a few inches and looking out. Then he moved to the windows above the sink to look out the side of the house.

Nicki's mouth had gone dry, as though she'd just swallowed a cup full of sand. Sterne looked nervous and his moves were edgy, making Nicki wonder if he was tweaking too. She didn't hang around meth heads, but she'd seen her fair share, and this guy acted like he was on something. She had to think, and she had to keep a cool head. So what did she need to do to get out of here alive?

All she could think of was one thing…that she had her cell phone in her pocket, and that could be her savior. It was already on and silent, so how could she use it to her advantage? She'd had friends who could literally send texts without looking at their phones—they could even do it in their pockets, and they were usually ninety-nine percent accurate (except that one time Brandy meant to type *cute boots* and instead typed *cute boobs*. Nicki had thought her old friend had decided to switch teams and that was her way of telling her until they had a good laugh about it later). Nicki didn't feel that adept at texting, but she had to give it a shot. One hand was already in her lap, so maybe she could try…

In the meantime, Sterne was pacing back and forth behind Melissa. He had the butt of the gun pressed up against his head as though it were an icepack and he had an injury. He was muttering through clenched teeth, but Nicki couldn't quite understand what he was saying. She used the opportunity to slide her phone out of her pocket. She didn't know if dialing 911 would do any good. Would the cops be able to figure out where she was and what was going on in time? And would they be able to do it before Sterne got wise? Or would they hang up, thinking it was just another dumbass butt-dialing?

She didn't trust them to do the right thing. Sean had seen to that.

But Sean…Sean she trusted. She pulled up her text window, her eyes darting from her hands under the table up to Sterne and then to Melissa, whose eyes were fixated on anything but Sterne or Nicki. For now, she was staring at the salt and pepper shakers on the table, and her eyes weren't budging.

Sterne stopped and turned, looking straight at Nicki. Had her eyes given her away? Nicki slid the phone back into her pocket and hoped her fingers would remember the right buttons to push. She already had Sean's number locked and loaded, the message ready to send; she just needed actual words in the message. She didn't know if she was glad right now that she'd never purchased a phone with a full keyboard or not. She didn't know that she'd be able to do this if she had a full keyboard, so she decided she was glad. She had to trust that her brain and thumb could make this work. In the meantime, though, she had to focus her eyes on crazy, crazy Sterne.

His eyes seemed even bigger than before. He pointed the gun at her again, his arm fully extended. He was across the table, though, so Nicki couldn't have grabbed it if she'd wanted to. Melissa could have, maybe, but Nicki didn't expect that. Sterne had stopped muttering, but his teeth were still clenched. "You that bitch that visited my brother last week?"

Well, Edwards had certainly called her a bitch, and she'd gone to see him. Visit, though…that sounded like a friendly word, and their exchange had been far from friendly. But this was no time to be a smart ass. "I had gone by his residence and tried to interview him. Last Thursday, I believe."

His anger didn't diffuse, but he did seem satisfied with her answer. "So why are you trying to track *me* down, bitch?"

She felt a film of perspiration spread out over her upper lip. The message was almost done. She just had to remain cool. She swallowed the nonexistent saliva in her mouth and then answered. "I'm not. Really. I'm just trying to report the facts for the readers of the *Tribune*."

He moved around the table to get closer. She stopped punching buttons and sat still. He dropped his voice.

"Then why you ask my old lady if she knows where I am?"

What could she say now to help him chill out? God knew. She could only try a half-truth, but she didn't want to get Melissa in trouble by telling him exactly what had triggered her question. "I don't know. I just thought maybe she would know."

"And why you think your readers need to know that shit, bitch?"

Nicki gulped again. "I guess they don't. I guess I was just curious myself."

"Fuckin' stupid." He started muttering and pacing again. Nicki punched the last button. She allowed herself to glance at the phone to make sure everything looked okay, then pressed send.

But *that* was fuckin' stupid, to use Sterne's words. He saw that she was preoccupied. "What the fuck you doin' over there, bitch?" He stormed back over to her chair. "Whatever you got in your pocket, take it out now." She took the phone and her car keys out and set them on the table. He grabbed the cell phone. "So help me, bitch…" He started pressing buttons, Nicki figured to check out the last calls she made. She felt overwhelming relief that she hadn't dialed the police, because she was certain that would have been the last call she'd ever made. Not that texting Sean would make this guy happy.

He turned around to the sink and dropped the phone in the glass of water. Had the message even made it out into the airwaves? There was no way to know. "Nice try." He strode back over to where Nicki sat, pulled back the fist with a gun in it, and hit her across the cheek. "Don't fuck with me." He started pacing again. He was trying to come up with a plan, Nicki thought. She just hoped it took him a while to figure out and that Sean had his phone on. More importantly, she hoped he knew what she meant by her message: *help. at m jacobs house*

But, since it was unlikely that Sean would ever get the message, she needed to figure out a way to stay alive and get out of there.

CHAPTER NINETEEN

NICKI BEGAN TO feel like a stressed-out meth addict just watching Sterne pace a rut in Melissa Jacobs's kitchen floor. In the past few minutes, Sterne hadn't said anything, had just continued muttering under his breath.

Finally, he sat at the table, legs splayed, hand gripping the gun as tight as a nervous mom might hold her three-year-old's hand in a crowded mall at Christmas. "We're gonna sit it out for a while. Once I'm sure the bitch didn't call the cops, we're outta here. You better pray you didn't, bitch, 'cause now you're a hostage. If you *did* call the cops, you'll probably be a dead hostage." Sterne said *probably* as though it only had two syllables, *prah-bly*, but he pronounced *bitch* perfectly.

She'd already figured out that her life was in danger. She'd assumed she was either immediate victim or long-term hostage. At least being a hostage, she had the chance of getting out with her body parts intact.

When she looked down, she could see that her cheek

had swollen. It hurt like hell. She had been asking herself why she'd thought becoming a reporter was such a great idea. She'd just thought it would be fun to see her name in print, to read her writing in the paper, have people around town talk about her insights. She hadn't stopped to think that she might actually be putting her life in danger or making people angry on a weekly basis. No one had warned her about that possibility. Then again, if the person training you is the Features reporter, she would have no reason to warn you about that. The worst thing that happened to the Features reporter was either getting bombarded with questions from kids at the school about what you ate for lunch or being bored to death by old people recounting their lives when they were young and cool. So Diane Glick couldn't have possibly prepared Nicki for this scenario. Diane's most dangerous day happened when she broke the heel on one of her shoes while reporting firsthand about the Boy Scouts building a new hiking trail by Cedar Creek.

Melissa had mentioned that she had sons there to worry about. Nicki wondered if the woman had made that up when she was trying to get Nicki to leave or if she really had kids and, if so, were they here? If they were, they were quiet.

Sterne kept pacing, pacing, pacing, and if Nicki hadn't been nervous before, she was now. The guy had a ridiculous amount of pent-up energy. The energy sparking off him could rival the Hoover Dam. Nicki knew, though, that he'd burn out at some point and then crash. Too bad that was far off in the future.

Not once since Sterne had entered the room had Melissa

looked up from the table. It was as though she were afraid to make eye contact, even with Nicki. Then again, had she looked at Nicki, Sterne would probably think they were communicating somehow. Nicki knew it was safer if they didn't look at each other. But that also meant that Melissa would be no help. In fact, she'd probably side with Sterne if it came down to it.

As the minutes ticked by on the worn white dusty clock on the wall, Nicki wondered if Sean had received her message. She had to assume that he hadn't...which meant she needed to figure a way out on her own. If she just got up and walked out, she had no doubt that Sterne would kill her. He had buck fever, and Nicki would be his target if she decided to run. No, thank you. She'd try another way.

Surely Sterne hadn't always been this psycho, but drugs could push a person there. Maybe, though, Nicki could try to tap into the rational part of Sterne. She could talk to him and perhaps get him to think straight.

Nicki took a few deep breaths, trying to think of a calm way to engage Sterne in conversation that could be productive. She decided to start with the most logical.

She took another deep breath and cleared her throat. Sterne had walked to the door and looked out the window again, making sure the curtain covered the glass when he was done. Nicki said, "Mr. Sterne, would you feel better if I interviewed you? You would be able to tell your side of the story. I wouldn't disclose your location or how we met; I'd just—"

Sterne knelt over so that his nose was close to hers. She saw that one of his front teeth was chipped. His voice was low, but she had no problems hearing him. "Are you fuckin' crazy? Do you really think I want to tell you anything? Do you think I want to share with the good citizens of Winchester just how I feel?" He exhaled. "The readers of your paper can go fuck themselves."

Tell me how you really feel. Well, it was obvious after spending this much quality time with Sterne that he and his brother Jason Edwards were definitely of the same stock.

And Nicki figured out in no time that the appeal to reason tactic wouldn't work. Sterne didn't care what people thought. Still, she wasn't able to let it go yet. "I was just thinking that if you're ever apprehended or if you were to turn yourself in and you went to trial, by having already told people your thoughts and feelings, you might have a sympathetic jury…which could translate into less jail time, maybe a reduced sentence."

"Were you not fuckin' listening, bitch? That's a stupid idea."

Nicki shrugged, trying not to let her fear show. That gun was too close, and she wasn't at an angle where she could even try to grab it. "Just a suggestion." Man, where was Carlos when she needed him? He'd already pulled this guy's psycho brother off her. But she knew Carlos was no doubt back to his own part of the world, possibly involved in gang activities as Sean had suggested.

No, Nicki was on her own now, and appealing to Sterne's logical side hadn't worked. She wasn't ready to give up, though. Sterne had resumed pacing back and forth, and Melissa was even more withdrawn. "Look, you know I didn't call the cops on you. Just let me go. You don't want to add murder or kidnapping to the list of charges the police have against you, do you? If you kill me, they'll lock you away for a long time, even if I'm not anyone important."

Sterne stopped pacing and seemed to consider her, but Nicki knew better when she saw the glint in his eye that wouldn't go away. Something was just not right about this guy. "That's if they know who did it. Why would they even suspect me?"

He had a point there, and Nicki could bluff, but she imagined that in this case a bluff would be more dangerous than the truth. She decided to just let it go. Obviously, this guy wouldn't listen to anything resembling common sense, so Nicki had to start thinking of another way out of this situation. How could she distract him so that she could find a way to escape? She knew she'd only have one chance. If she fucked that up, she'd be as good as dead.

Sterne resumed pacing until someone rapped on the door. Sterne stopped the exact second he heard it. He glared at both women and held the gun barrel up to his lips to indicate they'd better stay quiet. Nicki debated if she should yell, but again she sensed that Sterne had nothing to lose.

The person at the door knocked again. Sterne took a deep breath and approached the table. Melissa continued to stare at nothing, but his gaze alternated between the two women just the same. His voice was barely above a whisper. He hunched over so that Melissa had no choice but to look at him. "You're gonna answer the door and get rid of whoever's there. And not like you did with this fuckin' bitch." Nicki was sure Melissa was afraid, but the woman hid it well. "Got me?"

She nodded and stood. Sterne stood behind the door,

pointing the gun toward her, out of sight of the person at the door. Melissa opened the door a crack and looked out. She didn't say anything, but Nicki heard a voice that sounded sweeter to her than any other sound she'd ever heard. "By any chance, is Nicki Sosebee here?"

CHAPTER TWENTY

I'LL BE DAMNED. Sean had made it. Even if she hadn't put that man on a pedestal, he was her knight in a white t-shirt today. She wanted to shout out at him, but she knew better. Sterne would kill Melissa, Nicki, Sean, or even try for all three if Nicki was stupid enough to do that. Right now, Sean's best chance was putting two and two together. Nicki's car was outside and, now that Sean was here, he knew it.

Melissa didn't know what to say. She was the proverbial doe in the headlights, scared, pumped full of adrenaline, and paralyzed. There was no "fight or flight" in this woman. She was frozen. After what seemed like hours, though, Melissa managed to swallow whatever fictional lump in her throat had stopped her from being able to speak. Her voice squeaked, but she said, "Uh, Nicki who?"

From Nicki's vantage point, she could see that Sterne's neck was turning red. She didn't know what that meant, but she had her ideas about this guy. She imagined he was like one of those old-time thermometers in cartoons, the ones where—once heat was applied—the red flowed straight up in a rush and then burst out of the top, shattering the glass. *Volatile* was too mild a word for the guy.

Sterne pulled Melissa away from the door and slammed it. He shoved her back and stuck the gun out. His voice was low as he hissed, "Both of you, get over there!" His gun pointed toward the other end of the kitchen, near the doorway to the living room. "You say one word and someone will die."

Both women complied as Sterne opened the door. He held his gun in his left hand, just behind the door, ready for use. Sterne stuck his head in the small door opening and said, "You'll have to excuse my old lady. She didn't actually talk to the woman who came to the door earlier. Are you talkin' about that nosy reporter who came by a while ago?"

From where they stood, Nicki couldn't hear Sean's response. She did know that she and Melissa had an opportunity to get away from Sterne. From where she stood, she could see a big window on the street side of the living room, and maybe she could get Sean's attention that way. But, no, if she got Sean's attention, she'd also get Sterne's, and then someone would get hurt. No, there had to be a better way. There had to be a back door.

Nicki placed her hand on Melissa's arm and motioned toward the back of the house with her eyes. At first, Melissa scowled and seemed resistant, but then she nodded, sucking in a breath through her nostrils. The woman's pupils were wide and dark, and she *did* look like a doe—her light brown hair pulled back, dark eyes, slender nose. Once they were in the living room, Nicki asked, "Where's the back door?"

Melissa shook her head and started walking toward the back of the house. Nicki followed. The woman went down a small hallway and turned into a bedroom. And, sure as shit, there were two young boys in the room. They looked much like their mother—same brown hair, same helpless brown eyes. They were as quiet as a Sunday morning, sitting on the floor next to the bed. Both children appeared to be under five years old. Nicki felt an overwhelming sadness as she looked at the two little ones who had already learned how to survive in a house full of anger and abuse. Melissa sat down with them, apparently ready to accept her fate.

Nicki still whispered, but back here she could afford to be a little louder. She still heard Sterne's voice booming at Sean, so she knew he was distracted. "We've got to get out of here." The woman just looked at Nicki. Nicki didn't want to leave her, especially now that there were children involved, but she didn't intend to stay and play victim. "Where's the back door?" Melissa pointed toward the back of the house to the left and took a deep breath. Nicki said, "Come on. Let's go."

Melissa hesitated but then stood. "Mikey, Dale." Melissa picked up the littler guy and the older one took her hand. Nicki walked out of the room into the hallway first, then waited for Melissa. The woman continued down the hall toward the back of the house and followed it to the left, where it became a utility room complete with a beat-up washer and dryer, both old and not a matching set. The dryer was running, though, so at least they worked. The room had two unadorned windows, and Nicki could see sweet freedom in their near future.

Nicki stepped in front of Melissa to open the door so the woman wouldn't have to let go of her sons. The door was locked, but Nicki had it open in short order. She moved the door aside, then stepped out to hold the screen door so Melissa and her children could get out. Once outside, they walked down the concrete steps. Nicki saw that they were on the driveway beside the house; in front of them were the blue Chevy and burgundy station wagon she'd seen earlier. She knew that the window on the house just above the vehicles had to be the window to the kitchen. If Sterne was still occupied with Sean, the windows wouldn't be a problem, but if he was done and now wondering where the hell the women were, that window could prove to be a problem. However, Nicki didn't want to waste time wondering how to get out of there. She hugged the wall, her back up against it, hoping that position would make them hard to see, and began walking toward the front of the house. She looked over at Melissa, and the woman followed suit, her quiet little boys drinking it all in but saying nothing.

As they edged closer to the front of the house, Nicki heard Sean's voice again. She owed him a beer for this one. Fuck, she'd offer a blowjob too but she didn't think he'd take her up on the offer. She felt a palpable relief wash over her as they got closer to the front of the house, one step at a time.

She also heard, in the distance, a siren, and it was getting closer to their position by the second.

The foursome continued their slow trek to the front of

the house, and Nicki was finally able to make out some of Sean's words. "I don't buy that. Why would she just leave her car in front of your house?"

"I have no idea. She's nosy. Maybe she decided to talk to all the neighbors."

Nicki and crew had gotten as far as they could to the front of the house without getting to where they could be seen by Sean or Sterne, but they could hear everything clearly...including the siren that was now on the block. Only it wasn't one siren—it was two. Nicki could tell that by now. She looked to the right and saw her first glimpse of flashing red and blue...not one or two but three cop cars. And they all stopped right in front of Melissa Jacobs's house, blocking the road from any other vehicles.

Before anyone could get out of their cars, Melissa's older son broke free of her hand and began running toward the police cars. "Mommy, it's *Cops*," he said, pointing and running in that jolted, awkward way that only toddlers can.

"Mikey, no!" Melissa too began running, chasing her oldest son.

Jesus. All that hard work. Nicki stood for a second, not sure if she should join the melee as well or just stand back. Sterne was more likely to shoot her than his sons. But he was also more likely to shoot Sean. Nicki began walking toward the three of them but looking at the porch. Sean was turned toward the street as well, processing all the developments, and that's when Nicki saw Sterne, face now redder than ever, wrap an arm around Sean's neck and point a gun to his head.

CHAPTER TWENTY-ONE

NICKI HAD NOT asked Sean for his help to get him hurt, and yet that's what was happening right in front of her eyes. As though it were in slow motion, the action whirred around her, and Nicki just stopped in her tracks to watch everything that was happening.

Little Mikey continued running toward the street, Melissa still holding the smaller child, trying to catch the older one. The police were starting to get out of their cars. They were on high alert, hands reaching for weapons. Their sirens were now off but the lights continued to flash. The driver of the car directly in front of the house held a megaphone. Nicki didn't know if that was completely necessary, considering there wasn't much distance. Nicki looked up at Sean. He didn't see her or, if he did, it was in his peripheral vision. He didn't look scared or angry. He looked calm. Nicki didn't know what that meant exactly. It felt like a knife was twisting in her gut as her stomach acid resolved to eat her stomach itself with worry. *Sean, I'm so sorry*, she thought.

The police officer with the megaphone said, "Mr. Sterne, let the man go." So the cops *knew* whom they were dealing with. The budding reporter in her wanted to know *how* they knew and what had tipped them off to the goings on. Nicki doubted Sean had called them. He didn't trust the law, and she couldn't picture him deciding that calling 911 was a good idea. Nicki knew it must have been one of the neighbors. They'd probably seen Sterne one of the times he'd peeked out the window and decided to call.

"No fuckin' way, man." Sterne looked like he was ready to blow.

"Listen, Mr. Sterne, you don't want to hurt the man. Just let him go and no one will get hurt."

"Bullshit." Nicki could see from where she stood that Sterne was desperate. He started to back up into the house, pulling Sean along with him. While Sterne backed up, the gun still pointed at Sean's temple, Sean shoved his body to the right, slamming Sterne's arm into the doorjamb. He didn't drop the gun, but he did lose his aim. In the same instant, Sean twisted around out of Sterne's grip and punched Sterne straight in the nose.

Yep, it was his *BAMF* hand.

Nicki's body was stiff and immovable as she watched the action unfold. Sterne's gun went off, but the bullet went through the already-crumbling porch roof. Sean punched him in his face again and Sterne dropped to his knees. Sean kicked the gun out of his hand and the gun fell to the ground near the side of the house. Nicki was closest to it, but she didn't want to touch it.

The next thing she knew, no fewer than four officers

were rushing up to the porch, and Sterne was in cuffs, blood dripping down over his lips.

Sean leaned against the wall of the house, his face pale. One of the officers turned to him and started talking to Sean when another approached Nicki. "Miss, come with me please." Nicki saw Sterne being shoved into the back of a police car as an ambulance approached and parked behind the last police car. "Are you all right?"

It felt like someone else was controlling her body when she answered, "Yeah. I think so."

The cops had asked a lot of basic questions, wanting to know how everything had unfolded, but they wanted to get more formal statements from everyone after they'd checked out the premises. In the meantime, though, they wanted everyone examined by paramedics and needed the area cleared. Several officers were in Melissa Jacobs's house while Sean and Nicki sat on the curb next to her car. Nicki had seen Melissa's sons with her in the ambulance as a paramedic was giving her the attention she no doubt needed. Mikey was being entertained by one of the police officers who was showing him the walkie-talkie mounted on a shoulder clip.

Nicki had so much she wanted to say but no clue how to say it. She had to try. "Sean, I'm so sorry I got you involved in all this."

He looked over at her, a half smile on his face. "It's cool, Nicki."

She exhaled. "Yeah, but you could've gotten killed."

"Yeah, but I didn't."

She nodded, looking out at the two cop cars that were

now parked and no longer displaying their flashing lights. "Still...just accept my apology, okay?"

Sean was still looking at her and maintained his focus until her eyes finally met his. "Fine. But it's unnecessary. It's no worse than getting in a bar fight."

"And when's the last time you did that?"

He shrugged. "So I'm out of practice. I did all right, though."

That he had. "I just keep thinking that I'd probably be dead if you hadn't shown up."

"Well, stop thinking about it then."

"No, seriously, Sean. He had said that if the cops showed up, I was dead. But you came to the door, and we made our way out the back while he was distracted."

"Then stop fucking apologizing, Nicki. You texted me for help, and I did."

She scowled and pushed him with her shoulder. He was right. "Fine." He shook his head, smiling. "And thanks." He nodded. "Guess I should use this opportunity to get my own statements for the paper. A few impromptu interviews, and I'll have one helluva story." Her steno book and pen might have been in the house, but she had her car keys and fetched spares out of the backseat.

CHAPTER TWENTY-TWO

NICKI STROLLED INTO Sean's garage, grateful for the cool moist breeze she felt on her bare arms. It was the first rainstorm they'd had in two weeks, and she could hardly believe how much better it made her feel, both physically and mentally.

Sean was welding in the corner, causing blue shadows to dance around on the walls. His face was obscured by the helmet he wore, and he was leaning over, so Nicki knew he hadn't seen her. She wasn't concerned. She could wait.

He was playing Godsmack again, this time cranking some tunes off their first CD. As "Time Bomb" pounded through the garage, Nicki stood by the long table that ran along the entire east wall of the garage, looking at the framed articles Sean had hanging on the wall above the table. She'd seen them before—the picture where he opened his first shop and then the picture of him moving to a bigger location, the garage where she stood today. There were also other articles of some of his buddies, but there was a new one, she noticed. Sean had framed her first front-page article. She hoped, though, that she was holding one that would replace the one she was looking at right now.

This time her story was above the gutter, and her headline was large font. She was a *real* reporter now, and Neal had barely altered her words. Not only had she helped police discover where the elusive Michael Sterne was, she herself had seen the action, up close and personal. The hardest part of writing the article was keeping her personal feelings out of it. And the story was big. Sean had said he was going to start regularly subscribing to the paper, but she didn't know if he had started receiving it yet, so she didn't know if he'd seen today's paper. He might be surprised that, after the day they had yesterday, she'd actually not only written the article but had convinced Neal to extend her deadline a bit just so it could be in today's paper while the news was still fresh.

"Time Bomb" ended, giving way to the next song on the CD, "Bad Religion," and Nicki started tapping her finger on the table in beat to the music. The music was loud enough that she didn't hear when Sean shut off the welder. Instead, she heard him speak behind her. "Hey."

She turned around. Sean was placing the helmet down on a bench and walking over to her. He looked nice as always—snug blue t-shirt, faded blue jeans, black boots, blue bandanna around his hair, and ocean blue eyes framed by long brown lashes. "Hey, Sean."

"How are you today? Doing all right?"

"Yeah, I think so. You?"

"Business as usual." He walked over to the stereo and

turned the music down. "Actually, that's not true. I have a lot of catching up to do."

Nicki winced. That was her fault. "Guess I'd better make this quick then." She pulled the folded front page of the newspaper out of her jeans pocket. "Check this out."

Sean smiled. "Yeah, I saw it. Nice job. Your first big headline." She nodded, smiling back. "I'm proud of you."

He had no idea how good that made her feel. And she probably wouldn't tell him either. "Thanks, Sean."

He grabbed a white towel off the table and wiped his hands on it. "Did you ever find out who called the cops?"

She nodded. "Yeah. It was Mikey."

"One of Sterne's kids?"

"Yeah, his older one...the one who likes the TV show *Cops*. He'd grown up around Sterne and knew Sterne was violent, but Mikey had apparently been watching all kinds of *Cops* reruns over the past month. So when Sterne kept yelling about calling the cops, Mikey must have thought that was a good idea. Mikey ran into Melissa's bedroom and made the call to 911." Nicki shook her head. "They were so quiet, I didn't even know she had kids there until after you knocked on the door."

"Well, no harm done, right?" Sean looked up at the huge metal clock that hung over the middle garage door. "I think we should celebrate. How about I take you out to lunch?"

Nicki grinned. They *did* have lots to celebrate, and she couldn't remember the last time the two of them had gone to lunch together. Especially *just* the two of them...but she couldn't in good conscience not say anything. "But what about Kayla?"

"What about her?"

"Don't you want to invite her?"

Sean had pressed a button to lower one of the garage doors that was open, and it made a metallic noise as it worked its way down. "I don't think that would be a good idea."

Right now, Nicki's investigative reporter senses screamed at her but ultimately sucked, telling her nothing. Whatever Sean was trying to tell her wasn't quite sinking in. "And why not?"

"Because she broke up with me last week when I told her I didn't want to move in with her."

Hello. She felt like she'd just jumped in a fifty-degree-Fahrenheit lake and couldn't catch her breath. Sean started lowering the other open garage door and didn't seem to notice her surprise. That explained why Kayla hadn't come with him to her parents' house and why Sean was acting weird at Napoli with the guys the other night… Nicki finally said, "Why didn't you tell me before?"

He shrugged and turned around. "I don't know. I just didn't think about it. Not a big deal, really." He grabbed the "Be back at" sign that hung on the glass part of the door and moved the plastic clock dial. He walked over to the stereo and shut it off, then pulled the bandanna off his head and ran his fingers through his hair. Nicki wasn't surprised when it fell perfectly into place. Then Sean walked back to the door and opened it while switching off the lights. "You ready?"

Nicki willed her feet to move. Her first major headline ever and her best friend and biggest crush single again all in one day. She could barely believe it. She felt a smile spread over her face. "Yeah, I think I'm ready for just about anything." She strolled across the giant room to walk through the open door and relished Sean's warm arm around her shoulders as they walked to his truck beneath the cool sky.

THE END

ated by the tax system—are not based on income but on family structure—a reality that reflects just how much energy is in the system.

That's why I like this quote from the late Paul Samuelson, a Nobel Prize-winning economist, who said:

"The stock market has forecast nine of the last five recessions."

Wait, that can't be right. Actually, it is. The stock market is so volatile that it has falsely predicted more recessions than have actually occurred. It is a leading indicator, but not a perfect one.

GOT THE LIFE

ABOUT THE AUTHOR

Jade C. Jamison was born and raised in Colorado and has decided she likes it enough to stay forever. Jade's day job is teaching Creative Writing, but teaching doesn't stop her from doing a little writing herself.

Unfortunately, there's no one genre that quite fits her writing. Her work has been labeled romance, erotica, suspense, and women's fiction, and the latter is probably the safest and closest description. But you'll see that her writing doesn't quite fit any of those genres.

And Jade is a-okay with that!

Like Nicki? You can continue to follow her adventures in paperback (also available electronically for Kindle, Nook, and other eReaders).

#2 Dead
In paperback February 2013

Nicki's love life might suck, but her sex life is great. The only way both could be spectacular would be if her best friend Sean would look at her as more than just a friend. Nicki knows she's stuck in the friend zone, so she focuses her energies on her job. She's becoming a better reporter every day, so when her editor asks her to interview a local politician, Nicki is thrilled. But when the politician's secretary ends up dead, it's anybody's guess as to who did it. Nicki has a few ideas, though, and finds herself in deep trouble as she pokes her nose where she thinks it belongs.

#3 No Place to Hide
In paperback March 2013

The Tribune publishes an article warning the women of Winchester that there is a sexual predator on the loose in the streets of the town they once thought was safe. Danger doesn't stop Nicki, though, and it's not till it's too late that she discovers the criminal in the place she least suspects...and there's no one who can save her this time.

#4 Right Now
In paperback April 2013

Nicki is becoming a better reporter, so much so that her boss Neal leans on her more and more to get the good stuff. So when a rash of robberies hits the downtown Winchester area, Nicki is reporting the damage...and probably getting a little too close for the bad guys' comfort.

#5 One More Time
In paperback May 2013

Nicki notices there is a big problem with the homeless population in Winchester, and the local shelter doesn't have any more room for them. Nicki becomes irate when the City Council decides to do everything in its power to drive the homeless out of town, because she has other ideas.

#6 Lost
In paperback June 2013

The teenage daughter of a Winchester lawyer is kidnapped, and Nicki reports on the crime, hoping readers can offer clues to the authorities and find the girl...before it's too late. But what Nicki discovers leaves her horrified.

#7 Innocent Bystander
In paperback July 2013

Nicki, now disillusioned, realizes that she is but a tiny cog in a big machine, and she begins to feel like she's going to be swallowed up. As she opens her eyes to all that's around her, her life begins to fall apart. She loses her car, her apartment, and almost loses her job, all to circumstances beyond her control, and the bad guys have nothing to do with it. But, through adversity, Nicki learns what she's made of. She begins to dig deep into the underbelly of Winchester, and she finds that the drug trade isn't just for the junkies.

#8 Blind
In paperback August 2013

Nicki is angry. Now that she's seen what the people in power will do to keep their control, she knows she has to play it safe. She's threatened to topple their thrones and they're feeling nervous. But she's also feeling guilty about the murder of a prostitute whom she thinks she was responsible for, so she makes it her mission to help all the women of the night working in Winchester. And she does it the only way she knows how—by reporting what she's learned.

#9 Fake
Not yet available

Nicki has come to realize that she can't fix everything wrong with the world, at least not by confronting the bad guys head on, so she intends to educate people by tackling one small problem at a time. Now, there's a woman on city council who's growing a little too big for her britches and stirring up trouble in Winchester, dividing citizens into two clear sides—her side and the other—and Nicki plans to expose her for what she is.

Nicki's adventures aren't yet over…stay tuned for more!

Made in the USA
San Bernardino, CA
03 July 2014